It's All G

The Creation of Man
The Twelve Labours of Heracles
The Adventures of Young Theseus

Emily Templar

All rights reserved; no part of this publication may be reproduced or transmitted by any means, electronic, mechanical, photocopying, by future technology or otherwise, without prior permission of the copyright owner

First published in Great Britain in 2018
12 Churchill Avenue, Dawlish, Devon, EX7 9SB

Copyright © 2018 Emily Templar
Cover design copyright © Elemdee Design 2018
Illustrations copyright © Elemdee Design 2018

ISBN-13: 978-1975938291 (Paperback)
ISBN-10: 1975938291 (Paperback)

Created for e-book by Emily Templar Books EX7 9SB

Edited by Debbie Robbins

A Note from the Author

During my time studying for a BA in Ancient History, we were tasked to make something creative based on classical studies. In the opening seminar, we were asked what our project was, and why we were doing it. I stated, 'when I was a kid, I loved Greek myth, but I found the original writings heavy-going and fairly unreadable. But at the same time, I wanted the original stories. So, I was always really annoyed that there were never any books or anything for kids that didn't completely change or omit bits of the original myth'.

Choosing the story of Prometheus and Pandora, I set out on a mission to harmonise 21st century audience reception with ancient sources. I was determined to keep the myth as true to form as possible. I used every ancient source available, and narrative fluency was a challenge. At some points, the original sources are vague or contradictory. In these cases, I tried to find the most commonly-accepted narrative. If that wasn't possible, I would revert to Hesiod as the most comprehensive source. If that wasn't possible, I'd base my decision on narrative fluency. Some sources I had to completely ignore, such as Aesop, whose writings contradict huge parts of the other versions. Additionally, to retain fluency of the story, I had to add a few extended scenes, but they run closely to the original. For example, Prometheus stealing back the fire in a fennel stalk has very little detail in the primary sources, so I had to research across the mythos to find specifics on how to handle creating a scene based at the Olympian forge. I also had to characterise, where I regarded the mythos in its entirety, drawing personalities from the types of actions the gods did across the entirety of Greek mythology, as well as their personal chronologies and particular god interests.

The result is a form of Greek myth, which, inevitably, derives its characters and stories from my personal interpretation and creative liberties, but has a deep respect for the ancient stories whilst being hugely accessible to the modern audience, with humour and drama in equal measures. I hope to preserve the original myths as much as possible whilst being entertaining, and, if I'm lucky, to help inspire young readers to venture into the crazy, beautiful, and inspiring world that is ancient myth.

Many thanks to Dad. No Dad, no book.
Many thanks to Luke. No Luke, no pictures.
Many thanks to Debbie. No Debbie, no grammar, no spelling.
Many thanks to Hesiod et al. No Hesiod et al., no words.

The Creation of Man

'Don't you think it's cute?' the Titan Epimetheus asked his Titan brother, Prometheus.

In front of Prometheus was the creature that Epimetheus had created. The four-legged thing was gazing at them strangely. It looked ridiculous, with a long face and fluffy coat of fur. 'Err, what exactly is it?' he asked his brother.

'I think it could be called "sheep",' Epimetheus said happily. 'Don't you think it looks like a cloud? I was aiming for cloud.'

Prometheus looked at the sheep, and then at Epimetheus, who looked so proud of himself. He sighed. 'I wish you'd take this seriously,' he said. 'Zeus asked us to create all of the creatures that will live on this world, and you know how annoyed he gets when he doesn't like things.'

'I know, but come on, it's so cute!' Epimetheus said, and thought for a moment. 'Oh, I know, I'll give it big ears so it can hear lots of stuff!'

In a flash, the sheep had a pair of large ears.

Prometheus internally groaned. 'Really?'

'What, you think it's too much?' Epimetheus wondered.

Prometheus thought about answering that, but then looked at the sea of varying creatures, all quite strange-looking. It was a lost cause, he realised. 'Nah, it's fine,' he said. 'Anyway, are you nearly done?'

'Yeah, this is the last one,' Epimetheus said. 'Why?'

'I want to see what you provided humans with.'

Epimetheus blinked. 'Um, what?'

'You know,' Prometheus said, gesturing. 'That two-legged fleshy thing I gave you.'

Epimetheus paused. '... Oh, yeah,' he said eventually.

Prometheus gazed at him. 'You *did* give man something, right?'

Epimetheus paused for a second time. 'I was just ... getting to it.'

'What?'

'I forgot.'

'You *forgot!?*' Prometheus cried, annoyed.

Epimetheus looked as though he were about to cry. 'Well, I was just so busy making these fluffy things, and you brought in man a bit late, and I ...'

'You didn't give man *anything!*' Prometheus realised as he spotted man in amongst the motley crew of creatures. Man was still exactly as he'd delivered him – naked, shoeless, and without any means of defence. 'Look at him, he's pathetic!'

'Prometheus, I'm sorry!' Epimetheus insisted.

Prometheus sighed, trying to resist the urge to kill his brother. 'Okay. What can you give man now, then?'

'Um ...'

'Don't you *dare* say it,' Prometheus grated, his teeth gritted.

Epimetheus shut his mouth, his eyes wide.

'You've run out of things to give, haven't you?'

Silently, Epimetheus nodded.

'For the love of Zeus!' Prometheus cried, his head in his palm. 'So, man has absolutely *nothing!?*'

Still without a word, Epimetheus shook his head.

'Right,' Prometheus said, straightening up. 'I'm just going to have to do this myself then, aren't I?'

'How?' Epimetheus asked, confused. 'There's nothing left to give.'

Prometheus dwelled on that for a moment. 'We could give them fire,' he suggested.

Prometheus gave men fire, as well as the ability to learn, and the skills of metalworking and other sorts of crafts. He proudly watched as his creations grew and grew in number, living, learning, and completely at peace.

One day, Zeus called a meeting of the Gods on Olympus to discuss the current goings on, which, as per usual, included a feast. Everyone turned up, Prometheus included.

'I do love the meat of that cow thing your brother made, Prometheus,' Zeus said happily, eating a leg of beef. 'All this needs is some sauce! Maybe that horseradish plant.'

'Thanks,' Prometheus said, trying not to roll his eyes.

'This is why I've decided.'

'Decided what?'

Zeus looked to all the gathered gods. 'I have decided!' he announced to the gathering. 'Seeing as there's now so many of them, men must sacrifice part of their food to us, the gods!'

The gathered deities hummed and hawed approvingly. Prometheus, however, was incensed.

'You can't do that!' he squeaked.

'Pardon?' Zeus asked incredulously, turning to him.

'I said you can't do that!' Prometheus repeated. 'People without much food won't have enough to sacrifice!'

'Not my problem,' Zeus said, checking his nails.

'But ...' Prometheus began again, before realising that arguing with Zeus was probably fruitless. He could do nothing but remain silent, watching Zeus with hatred as the gluttonous god continued to work his way through the cow rump.

The Creation of Man

After the feast, Prometheus was pacing outside Zeus' chambers, waiting to be seen. He had a plan. He just hoped it would work.

After a few minutes the doors opened, and Prometheus entered. Zeus was sitting on his favourite godly chair, eating some grapes.

'Prometheus!' Zeus greeted. 'What brings you here?'

'You ...' Prometheus began, but quickly arranged his words a little better before starting again, 'I ... wondered if you wanted to play a game?'

Zeus looked delighted, clapping his hands together. 'Ooo, a game! I love games.'

'If I show you two types of sacrificial offerings, you can pick which one you'd like man to sacrifice ritually to the gods,' Prometheus said. 'Then whichever you pick you have to stick with for eternity. How's that?'

Zeus frowned. 'Oh, I'm not sure.'

'Go on. It'll be fun,' Prometheus coaxed him, smiling reassuringly. 'And no swapsies if you change your mind!'

'Okay then,' Zeus agreed.

'Cover your eyes, no peaking,' Prometheus said.

Zeus obliged, his hands over his eyes. 'What are you doing?' he asked.

'I'm just making the two choices,' Prometheus replied. As planned, he placed two piles. In the first, he hid succulent beef inside an ox's stomach, and in the other, he placed its bones inside a glistening exterior of fat. 'There we go. Open your eyes.'

Zeus looked at him, and then at the two piles. 'What do I do, again?'

'Pick the pile you'd like to be sacrificed to you. Whatever's in that pile is what we will have sacrificed to us for the rest of eternity.'

'Well, that's a little easy, isn't it?' Zeus wondered, getting up and walking over to the pile, which to his eyes, was appetising – glistening fat that was making Zeus hungry again. 'I pick this one!'

Zeus threw his hands into the pile of fat, ready to gorge himself, when suddenly he stopped, realising.

'Whoops, sorry,' Prometheus said, grinning. *'That's* the pile of bones.'

Zeus looked at Prometheus, and then the other pile, and back to the pile he had his hands stuck in. 'What?'

'You picked the bone pile. It was just covered in fat to make it look nice.'

Zeus looked horrified. 'B-b-but ... what's in the other pile?'

Prometheus split the ox's stomach apart and reached in, pulling out a handful of delicious red beef.

Zeus stared. 'I change my mind.'

'Oh no, no swapsies, remember?' Prometheus said.

'But ... this means men will eat all of the meat and only sacrifice to us bones and fat!'

'Yep,' Prometheus said happily.

'NO!' Zeus roared, looking at Prometheus with fury. 'You tricked me!'

'Hey, I gave you fair choice,' Prometheus said. '*You* picked the pile.'

Zeus gritted his teeth. 'But you *made* me pick that pile!'

'I wasn't even looking at it!' Prometheus protested.

'ARRRRGGGH!' Zeus screamed so loudly that Mount Olympus began to crumble. 'That's *it!* Men should not be more powerful than us! I RETRACT THE GIFT OF **FIRE!**'

Prometheus' face fell. 'You're gonna what now?'

'MEN WILL **NO LONGER** BE ABLE TO MAKE **FIRE!**'

Hanging around on Earth, Epimetheus heard the roar of Zeus shaking the ground as he took fire away from men. Seconds later Prometheus appeared, looking horrified.

'Zeus took fire away from men!' he told his brother, still shocked.

'Yeah, I, um, heard,' Epimetheus said.

'He's got no right!'

'He *is* ruler of the Gods,' Epimetheus pointed out.

'But men are going to suffer without fire!' Prometheus almost squeaked.

Epimetheus shrugged.

'This can't happen,' Prometheus said urgently, his hand on his head. 'I've gotta talk Zeus around ...'

And with that, he disappeared back to Mount Olympus.

Epimetheus stayed put, waiting patiently for Prometheus' return. He was just stroking the head of the thing he thought could be called a 'dog', when suddenly the sky seemed to crack open. The Earth shook as Zeus' voice boomed out, *'YOU WANT WHAT!?'*

Oh dear, Epimetheus thought. A few minutes later his brother was back, looking a little bit riled.

'That was a no, then?' Epimetheus supposed.

'Yeah,' Prometheus said. 'He said I could have it as a gift from him, but that's never a good idea with Zeus. Anyone who takes a gift from Zeus seems to get a life debt.'

'Yeah,' Epimetheus said, not really listening. 'So, what are you gonna do?'

Prometheus sighed. 'You know what? Those idiots up on Olympus need telling. Man needs fire, so I'm getting them fire.'

'But Zeus said ...'

'Zeus can go to Tartarus,' Prometheus interrupted. 'I'll go get fire from the forge at Olympus. Wish me luck!'

'Luck!' Epimetheus said as Prometheus disappeared.

The guards outside the forge of Mount Olympus were standing stoically by the entrance, creating a seemingly impenetrable wall. Prometheus, carrying a cornucopia of fruits and vegetables, walked straight up to them.

'Hi guys!' he greeted happily. 'How's it going?'

'Oh, so-so,' one of the guards said, smiling. 'Did you hear about Zeus and that thing with fire and men?'

'Yeah,' Prometheus said, nodding. 'Kinda ridiculous, isn't it?'

'Well, Zeus does have a short temper,' the second guard said. 'What are you doing here, Prometheus?'

'Me?' Prometheus asked innocently. 'Well strictly I shouldn't be doing this, but you guys work so hard and you do such a good job of guarding the forge, I thought, when does anyone ever thank *you*?'

He offered the cornucopia. The guards both looked delighted.

'Take ten minutes off,' Prometheus encouraged, smiling. 'Lunch break.'

The guards glanced at each other, and then each started grabbing handfuls of food.

'A lunch break?' the second guard asked, confused. 'I haven't had one of those in three millennia.'

'Well, you've got one now!' Prometheus said happily. 'Honest, head off. I'll guard the forge.'

'Oh, how nice!' the second guard said. 'You're the best, Prometheus.'

'I am, just don't tell Zeus that!' Prometheus replied, and everyone laughed. The guards left, and Prometheus checked the ransacked cornucopia. All that was left was a few apples and a fennel stalk.

He took the fennel stalk and dropped the container, the remaining apples spilling out and bouncing on the ground. With haste, he ran into the forge. Hephaestus and Athena weren't there, thankfully, so he went straight to the furnace and stuck in the fennel stalk. Within seconds, it had fire contained within it. He quickly dashed out again, and back to the world of men.

Zeus was angry.

Hera was becoming tired of her husband's constant pacing up and down on Mount Olympus. As well as interrupting what had supposed to be a relaxing afternoon between them, every stride he took caused the mountain to shake, prompting a little of her wine to spill from her glass with every ground-breaking stride.

Hera peered at him over the top of her copy of Goddess Monthly as he muttered unintelligibly to himself. 'Darling, could you stop pacing? You are giving me a headache.'

'Never mind your headache, Hera!' Zeus snapped. 'I am angry! I have never *been* so angry! That loathsome Prometheus has me riled, Hera!'

Hera sighed. They were back to the subject of Prometheus again. 'Yes, darling,' she murmured, resuming her reading.

'He has made a fool out of me, stealing fire for men!' Zeus bellowed, red in the face from anger. 'Do you know what I'm going to do?'

'Seek revenge, darling?' Hera supposed idly, still flicking through her magazine.

'Seek revenge, that's what!' Zeus cried. 'These humans now have fire! I should redress the balance of power! And I know exactly how!'

'Yes, darling?'

'I shall make a woman, who will bring about the woes of mankind through the box she holds! Or an urn! I haven't quite decided!' he declared. 'I shall have Hephaestus shape her form; Athena shall adorn her with the most elegant of dresses; Aphrodite shall make her beautiful; and Hermes shall instil within her a deceitful nature!'

'Of course, darling.'

'I shall then have her delivered to Prometheus' brother, Epimetheus! And he shall witness the dawn of the suffering of man first hand!' He stopped pacing, and looked at Hera. 'Are you even listening to me?'

'It's a lovely revenge plan, darling,' Hera commented, reading an article on the current trend in togas.

'I thought so,' Zeus grated, and stood up. He strode to the balcony, placing his hand defiantly on the balustrade as he gazed out beyond the mountain. 'GODS AND GODDESSES OF OLYMPUS, HEAR ME!' he roared, the mountain shaking. Hera quickly put her hand on her wine glass to keep it from falling over. 'ON THIS DAY WE SHALL SEND HUMANKIND ITS *WOES!*'

'WHAT'S HE ON ABOUT?' the voice of Demeter cawed from somewhere on Earth.

'IT'S PROBABLY ONE OF HIS REVENGE PLANS, AGAIN,' Poseidon replied from a nearby ocean.

'DIDN'T WE HAVE ONE OF THOSE *LAST* WEEK?' Aphrodite moaned from the other side of the planet.

'HERMES! ATHENA! APHRODITE! HEPHAESTUS! COME TO ME!' Zeus cried.

'BUT I'M WASHING MY HAIR!' Aphrodite complained.

'NOW!' Zeus roared so loudly that the planet had quite a violent tremor.

There was a collective, godly sigh as the deities muttered begrudgingly to themselves, and headed to Mount Olympus to act out Zeus' latest revenge plan.

'Happy birthday, Epimetheus!'

Epimetheus, having just arrived home from toiling in the fields, stopped dead in his tracks at the sight of the god Hermes standing there, outside his house.

'Oh, um, hey,' Epimetheus replied, confused. 'But it's not my birthday.'

'Never mind that!' Hermes said happily. 'Whatever today is, it's your lucky day, 'cause Zeus is sending *you* a gift!'

Epimetheus frowned. He was sure Prometheus had said something about accepting gifts from Zeus, but he couldn't really remember. It probably wasn't important. 'Um, but Zeus doesn't like me or my brother anymore. He locked up Prometheus.'

'Oh, it's all fire under the bridge, my friend!' Hermes assured him. 'No hard feelings, eh?'

'Oh,' Epimetheus said. 'Um ... what's the gift?'

'Handmade by the Gods of Olympus, a one of a kind article – I give you Pandora! Say hi, Pandora!'

Someone stepped out from behind Hermes, carrying an urn. Epimetheus looked at the person, and his jaw dropped.

'Hello,' Pandora said, smiling. The hair was perfectly arranged, cascading down the shoulders like a waterfall; the skin was soft and clear; the eyes were wide and bright; the dress was finely-made. It was the most beautiful creature Epimetheus had ever seen.

'She's all yours, Epimetheus,' Hermes said. 'Marry her! You know it makes sense.'

'Her?' Epimetheus echoed, confused.

'We call her woman,' Hermes told him. 'The first woman, all yours.'

For a moment, Epimetheus just stared at the beautiful woman in complete disbelief. 'M-marry her?' he stammered out.

'Yeah!' Hermes enthused, nodding.

Epimetheus continued to stare at Pandora. 'Um, hi,' he said awkwardly, blushing slightly.

'Hello,' Pandora said again in a voice like rose petals, giggling a little.

'Aww, isn't that nice,' Hermes said, grinning. 'Well, I'll leave you two lovebirds be. Oh! Wait, nearly forgot.' He pointed at the urn Pandora was holding. 'You two better not open that urn.'

Epimetheus frowned. 'Why not?'

'Just, you know, don't do it. Message from Zeus.'

'Why …'

'Toodles!' Hermes said, and disappeared in the blink of an eye, leaving Pandora, the urn, and Epimetheus together.

Married life was bliss.

As time went by, Epimetheus found himself more and more smitten with his wife. As well as being beautiful, she was also talented, especially at weaving. He loved her, and Pandora loved him.

The urn that they'd been warned not to open stood in their hallway, untouched. Both Epimetheus and Pandora passed it often, giving it a glance. Both were intrigued as to what was inside, but Pandora was the most curious. As she passed it, she sometimes found herself unconsciously reaching out to touch it. Each time, she quickly drew back her hand and forced herself to move away.

One night, Epimetheus was outside, and Pandora was alone in the house. After some weaving, she stepped out into the hallway to cross rooms. In the low light, she caught sight of the urn, seemingly glistening.

For quite a while, she found herself staring at it, wondering once again what was inside. Before she knew it, she was moving to the urn. She reached out to it, resting a hand on its surface. As always, it was vibrating a little and humming slightly.

She looked around for Epimetheus, but he wasn't close. She then looked back at the urn.

Open me, the urn seemed to say. *Else you'll never know what's inside!*

Pandora swallowed, and checked for Epimetheus again. Surely just a little peak wouldn't hurt?

Pandora slipped her thumb under the lid, took a deep breath, and opened it.

She screamed and stumbled backwards. From the urn came forceful jets of rancid black smoke. They fired up into the air, and with each jet Pandora felt them – ills, hard toils, heavy sickness – forcing themselves into the world. She realised in an instant that men, previously free of these torments, were now going to suffer.

Panicking, she stumbled forward and grabbed the lid, pushing it back on the urn. Immediately the outpouring stopped, just as Epimetheus came running inside.

'Pandora!' he cried, looking at her standing next to the urn. 'What have you done!?'

'Nothing! Absolutely nothing!' Pandora said unconvincingly.

'You opened the urn!'

'Well ...'

'Zeus said not to!'

THE CREATION OF MAN

'I'm sorry! I couldn't help it!' Pandora protested. 'It was just ...'

'You've released evil into the world!' Epimetheus said, horrified.

'I closed it! I closed it before they all got out!' Pandora insisted. 'I only let a *little* bit of evil into the world ...'

'Only a *little* bit of evil!?'

'I said I was sorry!'

Epimetheus moved forward, pushing her aside to look at the urn. 'There's still something inside,' he realised.

'Oh, Zeus,' Pandora cursed, biting her nails, worried. 'I hope it can't get out.'

Back on Mount Olympus, Zeus was roaring with laughter so hard that the pillars were cracking slightly.

Hera sighed, looking up from her new copy of Goddess Monthly. 'What is it now, darling?'

'She opened the urn!' he said, delighted.

'Did she now?' Hera murmured, uninterested.

'And all that was left in it was hope!'

'That's nice, darling.'

'Now to deal with that pesky Prometheus!' he said, standing up. 'For his trickery, and for stealing from me, I shall chain him to the rocks of Caucasus, and have an eagle feed on his liver every day for the rest of eternity!'

'I take it we're not having a night in, then?' Hera said, as he stormed out of the door. She sighed loudly, and poured herself another glass of wine.

The Twelve Labours of Heracles

Born as the result of an affair between the god Zeus and a mortal, Alcmene, Heracles had not only the strength of a God, but also the resentment of Zeus' shunned wife, Hera. As a stepmother, she had never been particularly nice to Heracles – never giving him birthday presents, not attending his chariot races, and occasionally trying to kill him.

Heracles' god-like strength sometimes came in quite handy. On one occasion, riddled with resentment for what Heracles represented, Hera had sent two serpents to kill him, but the eight-month-old Heracles had quite easily strangled them. On other occasions, it wasn't such a benefit. After his awkward rendition of a song had been heavily criticised by his music teacher, the young Heracles had lost his temper and bludgeoned him to death with a lyre.

As such, Heracles' wife, Megara, and their children, hadn't stood a chance when Hera had made him mad enough to kill them. After being cured of his madness, he'd gone to Delphi in despair, to seek advice from the god Apollo through the Oracle and ask how he could repent. Eventually he'd been told to seek absolution by offering his services to his cousin, King Eurystheus.

'Now, Hercules ...' King Eurystheus began after Heracles had finished his story.

'Heracles,' Heracles corrected.

'Whatever. Heracles, you have slain your wife and your children. You seek repentance for your crimes. It just so happens that I have many tasks that are impossible to complete. To gain freedom from the guilt of your crimes, you shall perform ten labours for me.'

'Sounds good,' Heracles said, nodding approvingly.

'Excellent,' Eurystheus said. 'First, you shall bring me the skin of the Nemean Lion!'

Heracles nodded again. 'Sure,' was all he said.

'You shall bring me the skin of the Nemean Lion!' Eurystheus repeated.

'Yeah, I heard you.'

'I said, the Nemean Lion!' Eurystheus insisted, obviously trying to get some sort of reaction from Heracles.

'Yeah, I've got it,' Heracles assured him. 'Nemean Lion. No problem.'

'Are you not afraid?' Eurystheus asked, confused.

'Nah. I've killed lions before.'

'But this is the Nemean Lion!' Eurystheus pointed out.

'So?'

'The Nemean Lion!'

'You don't have to keep saying it, I know. The Nemean Lion.'

'He's an idiot,' Eurystheus muttered to one of his associates.

'What?' Heracles asked. 'Can I go now?'

'Oh, er, yes.'

'Thanks,' Heracles said, turning. Then he stopped, and turned back. 'Wait, sorry. Where's this lion exactly?'

'The *Nemean* Lion?' King Eurystheus repeated questioningly.

'Yeah, but where is it?'

The King sighed. 'Zeus give me *strength*,' he moaned.

The First Labour: Heracles must slay the Nemean Lion

Heracles journeyed to the valley of Nemea, near Cleonae, where the lion dwelled.

As night drew in, he found himself in need of rest. He found a small house close to the valley, and knocked on the door. It was answered by a thin man with ragged clothes who introduced himself as a labourer named Molorchus. Molorchus hospitably invited Heracles inside, offering him nourishment as Heracles told Molorchus of his labour.

'Slay the Nemean Lion?' Molorchus repeated after Heracles had said it. 'You're bloody insane!'

'Am I?' Heracles wondered.

Molorchus frowned at Heracles' vague response. 'You *do* know what the Nemean Lion is, don't you?'

Heracles shrugged. 'Four legs, has a mane, goes "roar"?'

'It's the lion of the goddess Hera,' Molorchus stated. 'Trained by her. It's a plague to mankind. Son of the three-headed beast, Orthus, who is the sibling of Cerberus, the three-headed hound that guards the Underworld.'

'Really?' Heracles said, chewing thoughtfully on his food.

'It regularly eats the tribes around here. It's basically a king over Tretos, Apesas and Nemea. Only those driven mad by the Furies would ever attempt to kill it.'

'Oh,' was all Heracles said.

'You don't seem maddened by the Furies,' Molorchus remarked, gazing at him. 'So, what's in it for you?'

'I'm seeking repentance,' Heracles informed him. 'To do this, I've got to perform ten labours set by my cousin, King Eurystheus.'

Molorchus thought about that, and nodded. 'Then you're not mad. Well, not in that sense, anyway,' he said. 'I should make a sacrifice to you.'

'Oh. Why?' Heracles asked, baffled.

'Because that's the only way you're gonna get back alive.'

'Oh, no, it's okay,' Heracles insisted. 'Don't bother.'

'Please?'

'Honest, you don't have to.'

'Go on,' Molorchus encouraged.

Heracles could see that Molorchus wasn't going to give up. 'All right, look. If I don't come back in thirty days, you make your sacrifice to me. And if I do, then you sacrifice to Zeus.'

Molorchus frowned. 'But ...'

'Go on,' Heracles said, smiling.

Molorchus sighed. 'Fine.'

Heracles set out from the house of Molorchus the next morning, and eventually reached the valley of Nemea. He scoured the land until he finally found the ferocious-looking beast, with its thick tawny mane and dangerously large teeth.

For a while, Heracles observed its behaviour pattern. It would gorge itself on meat, and then, with the blood splattered around its face and its mane, it would make its way back to a cave. It was a pattern of behaviour that even the slightly intellectually-challenged Heracles worked out that he could use.

Heracles decided he would hide in the bushes outside the cave, waiting for his opportunity to strike. With his trusty bow and arrow in head, he knelt patiently. As the Nemean Lion approached, he drew back his bow string, instilling as much of his mighty power as he could, and fired it.

The arrow launched itself, powerfully and gloriously. The arrowhead, sharp and unforgiving, flew forcefully and precisely, and hit the Nemean Lion's left flank with a resounding thud.

Heracles watched, dumbfounded, as his arrow bounced harmlessly from the lion and fell to the ground. The Nemean Lion, startled, turned in Heracles' direction, letting out a blood-chilling roar as it threw back its head. Its face, teeth, and mane were covered in the blood of its latest tribe-themed meal.

'Uh oh,' Heracles muttered, and quickly launched another arrow, aimed straight at its exposed chest at the seat of its lungs. Again, the arrow merely bounced off its golden fur and fell between the Nemean Lion's massive paws. Panicking, Heracles began to launch another arrow, but the Nemean Lion finally spotted him. Heracles gulped as its dark eyes connected with his. It was like looking directly into Tartarus.

Then the Nemean Lion pounced.

Heracles dropped his bow and arrow, pulling out his club. As the Nemean Lion neared him in mid-air, its bloody claws out, Heracles swung his club with all his might, and connected with the Nemean lion's head with quite a loud "thunk!". The club split apart on its skull as the Nemean Lion stopped and whined a little. It staggered upright, and drunkenly made its way into its cave, stunned by the blow.

Breathing heavily, Heracles saw that the cave had two entrances. He needed to corner it. With a slam from his outrageously powerful fists, he punched one entrance, causing a rockslide to block it. Then, weaponless, he ran into the second entrance.

The Nemean Lion stood there, trapped. It roared with such ferocity that any normal man would have frozen on the spot in fear. Without thinking – as was usual with Heracles – he threw himself forward and wrapped his arms around the mighty beast's neck, and squeezed as hard as he could. The Nemean Lion struggled wildly, trying to throw Heracles off, but to no avail. It could do absolutely nothing as Heracles kept tightening his grip, his teeth gritted with the effort. Then, finally, the Nemean Lion's neck cracked, and the terrifying beast collapsed to the ground, dead.

Molorchus had been waiting patiently for thirty days, readying his sacrifice to the probably dead Heracles. It was a shame, he thought. Heracles had, admittedly, seemed a little stupid, but was otherwise a thoroughly nice chap.

He was about to begin the sacrifice when he suddenly spotted the figure of the Nemean Lion on the road, creeping slowly towards him. He yelped and dived behind a nearby broken cart, shaking with fear before he heard a familiar voice.

'Have you sacrificed anything yet?'

Molorchus dared to peek his head out and finally saw it wasn't the Nemean Lion, but was in fact Heracles, wearing the invulnerable skin of the Nemean Lion.

'Oh, not yet,' Molorchus squeaked, still shocked.

'Good,' Heracles said.

'You killed it ...!?' Molorchus realised.

'Oh, yeah,' Heracles replied casually.

Molorchus took a deep breath. 'You, Heracles, are a Hero. How by Zeus did you kill it?'

'Strangled it.'

'You *strangled* it?' Molorchus repeated, astonished.

'Yeah. How about this sacrifice, then?'

Hera watched, absolutely livid, as Zeus' son slayed her pet lion, took its skin, and wore it brazenly on his return to King Eurystheus.

'Why, that little ... son of a harpy!' she cried angrily. 'He dares to slay my lion and then saunter around in his beautiful skin!?'

Hera forced herself to calm down, taking deep, measured breaths. 'No matter,' she said. 'That annoying little illegitimate brat will die on his next labour!'

She sighed and made a decision. As the King of Beasts, her lion should live forever in the hearts of men. She dutifully placed the lion amongst the stars, and went to get a snack to eat. She had to have some nibbles to watch Heracles' surely inevitable death on his next labour.

The Second Labour: Heracles must slay the Lernean Hydra

King Eurystheus had screamed in fear when Heracles had sauntered in wearing the skin of the Nemean Lion, but had eventually calmed down enough to listen to how Heracles had completed such a seemingly impossible task. Hugely impressed, and a little annoyed, King Eurystheus ordered his second labour - to slay the Lernean Hydra.

Just as Heracles was preparing to leave, there was a knock on the door. Heracles opened it and, to his complete surprise, there stood his nephew.

'Iolaus!' he greeted happily, hugging his nephew. 'What are you doing here?'

Iolaus smiled. 'Just thought I'd see how the repentance thing's going! Heard Eurystheus had you doing this ten labours thing. Hey, loving the new lion skin style you've got going,' he added, pointing at Heracles' new attire.

'Thanks. Yeah, I'm just about to head out for the next labour, actually.'

'Oh?'

'I've got to slay the Lernean Hydra,' Heracles replied.

Iolaus raised an eyebrow. 'Isn't that the nine-headed hydra? The one with an immortal head?'

'I thought it was ten heads,' Heracles mused.

'Could be six,' Iolaus admitted, tapping his chin thoughtfully. 'Or maybe fifty. Anyway, you're really gonna kill it?'

'Yep,' Heracles replied.

'You're cool with that?'

Heracles shrugged nonchalantly. 'I've killed snakes before.'

Iolaus blinked. 'Well, this I've gotta see. I've got my chariot parked around the corner.' He gestured with his thumb. 'Need a lift?'

They discovered the Lernean Hydra on a ridge by the springs of Amymone. Leaving Iolaus with the chariot, Heracles made his way to a vantage point. This labour seemed like it would be much easier than the Lion. He lit his arrows and pulled back his bowstring. He waited only briefly before he aimed and shot the first burning arrow straight at the Hydra. As before, with infinite power and grace, the arrow carved through the air and slammed into the Hydra, and once again the arrow rebounded and fell uselessly to the ground. Heracles sighed.

The Hydra shrieked, and came out of cover, searching for the perpetrator. Without hesitation, Heracles launched himself at the Hydra, as he had done with the lion. The Hydra shrieked again, struggling, and managed to coil one of its necks around his feet. He swung wildly with his club, trying to take off some of the heads, but every time he took off a head, two new ones grew in its place. The heads were multiplying at an astonishing rate, and soon Heracles found himself unable to see hardly anything through the tangled mess of necks.

For the first time, Heracles wondered if his plan had been rather ambiguous, as a giant crab came sidling upwards, raising its pincer and snapping at his trapped foot. Wounded, and now very annoyed, Heracles roared and stamped his foot, crushing the giant crab immediately. But he was still trapped in the knot of necks.

'Iolaus!' Heracles cried, and whilst being whirled around, managed to catch an upside-down glimpse of his nephew running towards him. 'Help!'

'What d'you want me to do!?' Iolaus yelled.

Heracles rushed to think. 'Get some fire!' he shouted. 'Burn the stems of the necks when I cut off a head!'

'What!?

'Just do it!'

'Back in a minute!' Iolaus said, and ran to the nearby wood. Heracles had a jarring, shuddery view of Iolaus in the distance as he lit a part of the wood on fire. Shortly afterwards, he returned holding torches.

As soon as he had the striking advantage, Heracles raised his club and struck a head clean off. Iolaus immediately burnt the stem, preventing the head from regenerating. Heracles struck another. Iolaus burnt the stem again. They did this until only the immortal head was left, and Heracles promptly bashed it off.

'Woo!' Iolaus enthused, arms in the air after he'd burnt the stem and the body of the Hydra collapsed to the ground. 'Team Heracles and Iolaus!'

Heracles nodded, picking up the Hydra's immortal head. It snapped and hissed, trying to bite him.

'Oh, freaky,' Iolaus commented, staring at the head. 'What are you gonna do with that?'

'Mantelpiece,' Heracles replied.

Iolaus raised an eyebrow. 'Uh, you're not serious, are you?'

'Why not?' Heracles asked, just before the head tried to snap at him again and came quite close.

'I'm as much in favour of trophies as the next guy, but I think cleaning your mantelpiece is gonna be a bit difficult with that on it,' Iolaus pointed out.

'You're probably right,' Heracles conceded, and looked around the terrain for some inspiration. He spotted a heavy rock. He sauntered over, throwing the rock aside with ease before punching the ground with his free hand to create a hole, and dropping the head inside. The head snapped some more before Heracles covered it with mud and placed the rock over the buried head. 'Done,' he concluded.

'Back to Eurystheus?'

'In a second,' Heracles said, looking at the corpse of the Lernean Hydra. 'Got an idea.'

'Another one? You're on fire today,' Iolaus commented as Heracles stooped to the corpse and cut it up. He dipped his arrowheads in the deadly venomous hydra blood, and nodded, satisfied.

'Another mighty creature dead!' Hera shouted angrily. 'Is there nothing that can kill this fool!?'

Next labour, she thought to herself. The next labour would bring the wrath of the gods down on the unaware Heracles. Surely, *surely*, he would meet his end?

In the meantime, she thanked the crushed crab for his service to her in the fight against Heracles, and placed it and the Hydra among the stars.

THE THIRD LABOUR: HERACLES MUST RETRIEVE THE HIND OF CERYNEIA

King Eurystheus was quite astonished to see Heracles back in his presence with such a heroic story to tell, accompanied by that irritating little nephew of his, Iolaus. King Eurystheus was already annoyed by the mere presence of the two long before they told their story. As such, when they finished, King Eurystheus was shaking his head.

'Well, that's no good, is it?' he said.

'What's no good?' Heracles asked, confused.

'You had help on that labour! I never said you could get someone to help you complete these labours!' the King declared.

'You never said I couldn't,' Heracles countered, frowning.

'Yes, I did!' King Eurystheus insisted.

'No, you didn't.'

'Yes, I did! It's a thing! It's always been a thing!'

'Hey, you can't just change the rules,' Iolaus protested.

'I'm not changing the rules! He must not have been listening properly!' King Eurystheus declared.

'For Zeus' sake,' Iolaus cursed under his breath.

'Heracles, for your next labour, you must bring me the Hind of Ceryneia!'

Iolaus frowned. 'But that's a deer sacred to the goddess Artemis,' he pointed out. 'She'll kill Heracles if he touches that deer.'

'I don't care,' King Eurystheus said. 'Bring me the Hind of Ceryneia!'

'Okay, okay,' Heracles said. 'Just tell me where to find it.'

'The clue is in the name!' the King responded, his head in his palm.

As he set off to kill the hind, Heracles mused that having one goddess' wrath directed at him was enough, and that maybe he should refrain from annoying any others. The King hadn't specifically stated that the hind should be dead on arrival, so Heracles decided quite quickly that he would bring it back to the King alive, to avoid the fury of Artemis.

Therefore, what should have been quite easy was made quite a lot more time-consuming by his reluctance to hurt the hind. The defenceless deer of Artemis with its bronze hooves and golden horns was frighteningly easy to locate, and many a time Heracles could have killed it quite swiftly. But he didn't.

For a year, he followed the deer across the land from Oinoe to the mountain of Artemisium, trying to capture it without causing it any harm. When the hind crossed the Ladon river, he found his moment. He raised his bow and arrow, and fired a shot straight into one of its hooves.

On impact, it let out a strange, pathetic noise and staggered, falling. Heracles moved in to pick it up and hoist it around his shoulders, and rushed as quickly as he could through Arcadia to get back to King Eurystheus. Unfortunately, he was noticed.

'Heracles!' the voice of Artemis suddenly called, as she and the god Apollo appeared in front of him. 'What are you ...' - her eyes snapped to the animal he was carrying - 'that's my deer!'

'That's Artemis' deer!' Apollo stressed.

'Yeah, um, I'm sorry,' Heracles said, a little bashful.

'You tried to kill my deer! Apollo! Look! He's got my deer! Why, I oughta ...'

'I'm sorry!' Heracles repeated. 'I didn't want to hurt it, but ...'

'YOU **SHOT** IT!' Artemis screeched loud enough to quake the ground around them.

'It's not dead!' Heracles protested.

'AND THAT MAKES IT *OKAY* THEN, DOES IT!? IT WAS A **GIFT!!!**'

'I'm sorry!' Heracles said for the third time. 'King Eurystheus asked for the hind of Ceryneia!'

'Oh, wait! You're doing that labours thing, aren't you?' Apollo realised.

Artemis looked as though she were about to explode into a perfect godly mess. 'Oh, I'm having a word with that Eurystheus! Let me at him! *LET ME AT HIM!*'

'Artemis,' Apollo said, resting a hand on her arm. 'Eurystheus didn't tell Heracles to kill the deer to complete the labour. How about you let Heracles take it to Eurystheus alive? Then you can heal it.'

Artemis paused, blinking back her tears. 'Oh.'

'Then there's no biting or smiting, right?'

'... Right.'

'Everyone wins!'

'Yeah ...'

'All good?'

Artemis nodded, clearly struggling to hold back tears. Apollo gestured with his head to Heracles, indicating he should make his way slowly and quietly past the upset goddess. Heracles obliged, almost tip-toeing his way.

Finally passing the deities unscathed, Heracles made his way back to King Eurystheus.

'Artemis, you fool!' Hera screeched as she watched events unfold. 'Why are you being so reasonable!? Stop being reasonable!'

Hera, once again, found herself taking a few deep breaths to calm down. The next labour, she told herself, and went to retrieve more snacks.

THE FOURTH LABOUR: HERACLES MUST CAPTURE THE ERYMANTHIAN BOAR

'Well, that took you a while,' King Eurystheus commented when Heracles presented the hind to him. 'I was beginning to think a simple deer had outwitted you. Though, that wouldn't be too hard, would it?'

Heracles missed the insult. 'What's my next labour?' he asked.

'Not so fast, *Hero*,' King Eurystheus said, the latter word completely lacking sincerity. 'This hind is not dead. I specifically said that –'

'Actually, you didn't,' Heracles pointed out. 'You said "bring" the hind, not kill it.'

King Eurystheus quietly cursed. The dimwit *had* been listening. Somewhat infuriated, he stood up from his throne and took a deep breath to inflate himself slightly. 'Right! This time I want the Erymanthian Boar! And I want it *alive!* See?' He looked to all his servants in the room. 'I am saying *alive!* Someone write that on a papyrus!'

'Sure thing,' Heracles said, nodding and turning to leave. Then he stopped, turning back to King Eurystheus. 'Sorry, where …'

'Erymanthos!' the King yelled.

Heracles travelled to his destination, and eventually came across two mountains, one of which he knew was Erymanthos, but puzzled as to which one it was. Slightly confused, he reached the base of the first mountain, and noticed an entrance of some kind in the rock. Someone lived here. He knocked on the door, and a centaur answered.

'May I help you?' the centaur asked, surprised.

'Sorry to bother you, but can you tell me what mountain this is?' Heracles asked.

'This is Mount Pholoe,' the centaur informed him.

'Oh, so it's not Erymanthos?'

'No,' the centaur said. 'That's one mountain over.'

'Ah, my mistake, sorry,' Heracles said with a smile, and turned to continue his journey.

'Forgive me, but why do you travel to Mount Erymanthos?' the centaur asked, stopping him mid-turn.

'I've gotta capture the Erymanthian Boar and take it back to Tiryns for King Eurystheus,' Heracles replied.

The centaur frowned. 'Uh, he does *know* you're doing that, I hope?'

'Oh, he told me to,' Heracles assured him.

'I'm confused,' the centaur admitted.

'I'm performing ten labours to repent for murder,' Heracles answered. 'King Eurystheus ordered me to capture the boar alive.'

'He has sent you on a suicide mission,' the centaur said. 'Turn back before you die.'

'Sorry, err, what's your name?'

'Pholus,' the centaur replied.

'Oh. Are you named after the mountain?' Heracles wondered.

'Why, the mountain's named after me,' Pholus replied boastfully. 'What is your name, traveller?'

'Heracles.'

Pholus instantaneously looked delighted at his name. 'Heracles, please be my guest. You should rest before you attempt your great task. I have meat, and some wine.'

Heracles shrugged nonchalantly. 'Okay, sounds fun,' he said, and stepped inside Pholus' cave dwelling.

After pottering around in another room a while, Pholus emerged with roast meat for Heracles, raw meat for himself, and a tall jar.

'This jar of wine has been buried in the earth,' Pholus informed him. 'It has been passed down through four generations, left by god of wine, Dionysus, himself. I was told once that when a man named Heracles visited me, I should open this wine for him.'

'Oh, that's nice,' Heracles said, smiling.

Pholus beamed. 'I must say, I have always wanted to try this,' he admitted, and opened the jar. Immediately the potent, sweet odour of the strong old wine filled the cave. 'Oh, how sweet smelling it is,' Pholus commented, and reached forward to pour Heracles some.

Suddenly Heracles and Pholus jumped in alarm as the door burst open. In rushed a herd of centaurs, their eyes crazed.

'What is this sweet smell!?' one of them cried.

'We should have this wine!' another yelled.

Pholus screamed and hid behind a drape as Heracles stepped forward, his hands curling into fists to protect his host.

'I'm warning you, stay back or I'll -'

'Get it!' another screamed, and they charged.

With infinite calm, Heracles armed himself with wood from the fire and showered the assailants with the brands. The beings with the swiftness of horses and the strength of two men were quite a challenge, but Heracles was stronger. He overcame each of them in turn, in a true show of his demi-godly strength. He forced the centaurs out of Pholus' house and into the clearing, firing arrows and whirling his fists. More and more crazed centaurs arrived, armed with everything from rocks to firebrands to axes. A couple even carried – to Heracles' consternation – a couple of fully-grown pine trees still with their roots, attempting to ram him.

Heracles continued to fight, even as the cloud nymph Nephele aided the centaurs by causing it to rain. That was not a problem for the four-legged centaurs, but caused Heracles to slip and slide all over the place. But he fought on unyielding, eventually killing the majority of them. When it became clear they were going to lose, the surviving centaurs quickly fled. The rain cleared, and Heracles was left standing amid the bodies of fallen centaurs.

Pholus finally emerged from hiding. His face fell. 'Oh,' was all he said at the sight of so many of his kind lying dead.

'Err, I'm sorry,' Heracles said, feeling a little awkward.

'No, no, they were enraged beyond reason,' Pholus assured him. 'You fought with such strength and calm, Heracles, and you must be admired for that. But I should give them all a burial, as they are my kindred.'

Heracles nodded. 'I'll go and, err, clean up,' he murmured, gesturing vaguely at his mud-soaked sandals and legs before he left.

As Heracles left, Pholus moved to one of his dead kindred, noticing a single, slim arrow poking out of their flank. He pulled the arrow out.

'Oh, how could such a small thing kill one so mighty?' Pholus wondered aloud, marvelling. But as he made to cast the arrow aside, it slipped from his hand and landed, point down, in his foot. 'Whoops,' he said, and immediately died.

A few minutes later, Heracles re-emerged, a lot cleaner. 'Oh, by the way, my arrows are coated in Lernean Hydra poison, so don't …' His voice trailed off as he saw Pholus lying dead next to the other centaurs, an arrow sticking out of his foot. 'Ah,' was all Heracles said.

Heracles dutifully buried Pholus in a magnificent ceremony at the base of Mount Pholoe, with the mountain itself serving as the headstone of the hospitable centaur. Once Heracles was done, he proceeded onwards to Mount Erymanthos. He still had a boar to catch.

The mountain was covered in snow and trees, and finding the boar proved a little difficult. He eventually routed it out of the trees by shouting as loudly as he could, and chasing after it into the heavy snow. It didn't take too long before the boar's energy was sapped by running through the deep snow, allowing Heracles to catch up and capture it with a noose quite easily.

Triumphant, he took the boar and headed back to King Eurystheus, the labour completed.

THE FIFTH LABOUR: HERACLES MUST CLEAN THE STABLES OF AUGEAS

King Eurystheus screamed a very high-pitched scream and promptly jumped into a conveniently-placed man-sized bronze jar when Heracles presented him with the living, captured boar.

'Get out!' he screamed, his voice muffled in the jar. 'Get him out right now!'

Heracles blinked. 'Um, what are you doing?'

'Get *out!*' the King repeated, a hand emerging out of the jar and pointing frantically towards the door. 'Release that boar and never bring the results of your labours in here again!'

Heracles sighed. The king was beginning to irritate him somewhat. 'But you said ...'

'Get it out!' King Eurystheus squeaked.

'I need my next labour,' Heracles protested.

'Err, um, err ... clean out King Augeas' stables!' the King said quickly.

'That's not a labour,' Heracles complained. 'That's farm work.'

'Oh, no good enough for you, Hero!? You must clean them out within a *day!* You hear that? Within a *day!* No help! No nothing!'

Heracles was feeling a little bit cheated as he made his way to Elis, where King Augeas ruled. Killing lions and capturing boars was one thing, but cleaning up what came out of the back of animals within a time limit was hardly a tale that would hold much glory two thousand years down the line.

His annoyance at this complete lack of a challenge was so much so in fact, that when he finally had an audience with King Augeas, he'd already decided that he would be getting a little more out of this labour than maybe King Eurystheus had in mind.

'King Augeas, I am Heracles,' Heracles declared to the King. 'I believe you have a problem with your ass.'

'I beg your pardon?' King Augeas asked incredulously.

'Your donkey?' Heracles amended questioningly. 'I hear your stables are filled with dung.'

'Oh,' the king realised. 'Yes, they are. And I have cattle, not donkeys.'

'My mistake,' Heracles said shrugging. 'I've got a great deal for you.'

'What deal?'

'I'll carry out all the dung for you within a day, but as payment I want in return a tenth of your cattle.'

'Are you serious?' the king asked, incredulous.

'Yes.'

'That is ridiculous.'

'Then you don't want your stables cleaned?' Heracles wondered.

Augeas sighed. 'Okay, okay. Since you seem to be so sure of your dung-cleaning abilities, I promise if you manage this, I shall reward you with a tithe of my cattle.'

'Err, a tenth,' Heracles corrected.

King Augeas frowned a little. 'Err, a tithe *is* a tenth,' he said.

'Oh, is it? Great,' Heracles said happily.

'But as proof, you need a witness,' the King said, and gestured to a spotty teenager on his left. 'Take my eldest son, Phyleus, with you to watch this.'

'I can't believe you're gonna do this,' Phyleus said as they neared the stables. 'No one's ever done this before. You must really like shovelling dung, dude.'

Heracles shrugged nonchalantly. 'It's not hard, just a bit stinky. What's a few cattle?'

'Err, you do know how many cattle my dad *has*, right?'

'Err, no?'

'Well ...' Phyleus stopped by the stables and pointed at the landscape. Heracles followed the boy's indication, and stared. From where they were standing, they could see a huge cattle yard rolling out across the landscape. Almost every inch available seemed to be populated by cattle, to the point that Heracles couldn't even see the ground. The stables they were standing next to towered over them, stretching for at least a couple of miles. Phyleus then opened the door to the stables, and the smell of rancid dung hit Heracles like a Titan punching him in the face. Piles and piles of dung were stacked up like mini mountains down the entire length of the stables, as though something unfeasibly large and with an upset stomach had passed through.

'Hmm,' Heracles said, scratching his head after he'd managed to stop coughing at the disgusting smell.

'You didn't know?' Phyleus asked, hand on his nose.

'No one mentioned it,' Heracles replied.

There was a long silence.

'Err, so you gonna do this or what?' Phyleus wondered.

Heracles scoured the landscape, searching for some inspiration. Eventually his eyes landed on a large river, snaking its way past the stables, with another one running quite close.

'What rivers are those?' he asked Phyleus.

'The Alpheus and the Peneus,' Phyleus answered promptly, pointing at each in turn.

'Right,' Heracles said, and got to work. With his club in hand, and Phyleus as witness, Heracles made a breach in the foundations of the cattle yard before heading to the rivers. Phyleus watched, astonished, as Heracles used his strength to divert the rivers away from their natural course and straight into the cattle yard.

The combined waters of the Alpheus and the Peneus formed a powerful torrent and went straight through the stables, taking every single piece of dung in its wake.

When Heracles and Phyleus returned to King Augeas, the king did not look at all pleased to see them. Both, however, were far too happy to notice the king's grumpy face.

'Dad, he did it!' Phyleus said, beaming from ear-to-ear.

'Did he, now?' the king asked dryly.

'You should've seen it!' Phyleus said, enthused. 'He diverted the rivers and it cleaned the whole place out! It was awesome! You're the best, Heracles!'

Heracles tried not to look too full of himself, casually checking his nails.

'I thank you, Heracles,' the king said in a tone of voice that conveyed anything but appreciation. 'Be on your way.'

Heracles frowned. 'Wait ...'

'You owe him the tithe of the cattle!' Phyleus stated, confused.

The King adjusted his crown, staring fiercely at Heracles. 'I was eating with some of my associates earlier, and you know what I discovered about you, Heracles?'

'Just how great he is?' Phyleus asked, bouncing on his toes eagerly.

'He is in the service of King Eurystheus!' King Augeas declared, pointing at Heracles. 'This was a labour commanded by him! This man had the *audacity* to ask for a payment from me for a repentance labour!'

Phyleus' jaw dropped, and he looked at Heracles. 'Really?' he asked his new friend.

'Well, um ...' Heracles began, looking a little bashful, '... kind of.'

Phyleus thought about that, before he shook his head and turned back to his father. 'Hey, Dad, that doesn't matter. You promised to pay him, so you've gotta do it.'

'I made no such promise,' the king replied calmly.

Heracles sighed a little. Kings were all the same. 'You said that you promised to ...'

'I did not,' the king interrupted. 'Now be gone!'

'Dad!' Phyleus protested. 'I was there! I heard it! You said it!'

'I will hear no more of this!' the king cried.

'Heracles ain't letting this go!' the teenager protested.

'Then we shall let the arbitrators decide!' the king said. 'See you in court, Heracles!'

Arbitration had been going quite well for a while.

King Augeas' representatives had laid out his case very convincingly, and at the end of it he was looking very smug, as though it had already been won. What he hadn't been expecting, however, was that as a witness Heracles would call the king's son, Phyleus, to testify against his father. After that, things had gone rather pear-shaped for the proud king, so he had immediately stopped the arbitrators voting, and banished both Heracles and his own son from his kingdom of Elis.

Phyleus had protested, but his father hadn't cared. Heracles, who'd grown to quite like the teenager, swore to the king's face that he would one day return with an army, and left Elis with Phyleus in tow. Needless to say, the arbitration wasn't completed, and Heracles didn't get paid.

'What will you do?' Heracles asked Phyleus as they passed the border of the kingdom that had been the teenager's home for so long.

'Travel north, I guess. I've got people in Dulichium I can live with,' the teenager said. 'What about you?'

'I've got labours to get on with,' Heracles supposed. 'But I promise, Phyleus, once I'm finished, I'll come back.'

The Sixth Labour: Heracles must chase away the Stymphalian Birds

News travelled fast between Kings, and by the time Heracles returned to King Eurystheus, he'd already heard of Heracles' attempt to gain payment for the labour.

'Tut, tut,' the King said, shaking his finger disparagingly at Heracles. 'Taking payment for a labour does not look good on your record, Heracles.'

'You didn't say anything about ...'

'I'm not getting into this again!' the king complained. 'I will remember this, Heracles!'

Heracles narrowed his eyes. He really was becoming increasingly irritated with his boastful, self-loving cousin. With each labour and every year that passed, Heracles was becoming stronger and wiser, but his cousin remained the little sod he'd always been. 'Fine, okay. What do you want me to do next?'

'The next labour you will find *impossible,*' the king stressed. 'You must chase away the Stymphalian Birds!'

'Chase away birds?' Heracles repeated disbelievingly.

'Yes, that's what I said.'

'Are you running out of ideas?' Heracles asked seriously.

'The Stymphalian birds are numerous and man-eaters! They're horrible things, as big as cranes, with sharp beaks and these little evil beady eyes!' the king replied with all the appropriate mimes.

'I'll take your word for it,' Heracles said, rolling his eyes and leaving.

Heracles travelled to Arcadia, directly to the lake known as Stymphalis, located in a dense growth of trees. There he saw the man-eating birds, milling around in the cover the trees provided, trying to avoid the wolves.

Despite the apparent ease of the labour, Heracles realised the problem as he cast his gaze over the birds. There were so many of them lurking under cover, and he needed to flush them out somehow without becoming their dinner.

He was considering this problem at length when the goddess Athena appeared next to him.

'Hello, Heracles,' she greeted. 'What you doing?'

'The sixth labour,' Heracles replied.

Athena looked a bit confused. 'Wow, still on your labours?'

'Yeah,' Heracles replied, still scanning the flock of birds, trying desperately to think of a solution.

She clearly realised he was a little distracted. 'What's this one about?'

'I have to flush out these birds, but I don't know how,' Heracles answered, pointing at the flock.

'Oh,' Athena said, thinking about that for a moment, before nodding. 'I've got an idea.'

And with that, she disappeared in a godly whirl of colour. Heracles barely acknowledged that, moving around the perimeter of the lake to a better vantage point next to a mountain. Seconds later, Athena reappeared holding a pair of bronze castanets. 'Hephaestus, god of the Olympian forge, gave these to me,' she said. 'Maybe you can use these to scare them out.'

Heracles frowned a little, taking them. 'Thanks,' he said, and clashed them together. It was loud, but the birds hadn't seemed to have noticed. He turned back to Athena, but she was already gone.

Staring at the castanets in his hands, Heracles pondered what to do next. He then looked to his left, and realised he was standing at the base of a mountain that overhung the lake.

An idea crept into his head.

He ascended the mountain to reach a good vantage point, readying his bow and arrow. Then, with all the force he could muster, he clashed the castanets on the mountain.

The resultant rumble was deafening. The birds shrieked and a few of them flew up into the air, trying to get away from the noise. Heracles loaded his bow, and took a few shots at a few of the fleeing birds. Several fell down, dead, stirring a few who had remained in the lake to fly up and flee with the rest of their kind, all of them unable to determine where the arrows were coming from. When just a few remained,

Heracles promptly ran down the mountain, screaming and clashing the castanets together. Very soon the lake was clear, and the birds were just a flock in the distance.

The Seventh Labour: Heracles must fetch the Cretan Bull

King Eurystheus was getting a little more creative with his labours again, which, frankly, Heracles appreciated, after the nature of his previous two.

After he'd chased away the Stymphalian Birds and returned to King Eurystheus, he was ordered to retrieve the Cretan Bull. He promptly boarded the boat to the island of Crete, where the bull dwelled. Much to his delight, Heracles found he was starting to be recognised, and even had a clutch of fangirls and fanboys sailing with him, eager to hear about his next labour. Luckily, there was a knowledgeable teacher from Athens on hand to explain the origins of the ferocious bull.

'Some say that King Minos of Crete once promised Poseidon that he would sacrifice whatever the god sent out of the sea, and Poseidon sent a beautiful, strong bull. But King Minos thought the creature so magnificent that he couldn't bring himself to kill it. So he took the bull into his herd, and sacrificed a different bull in its stead. King Minos' actions infuriated Poseidon, and in response he made the bull wild and dangerous. It now roams the island of Crete, killing all those who dare to stand in its way.'

'And you're going to catch it?' a fangirl asked, batting her eyelashes at Heracles.

'You're so strong!' a fanboy gushed.

'Well,' Heracles began, shrugging back his shoulders to show off his muscles, 'it's on the to-do list.'

'Oh, you're so dreamy,' the fangirl purred.

'Can I have your autograph?' the fanboy asked, holding a bit of papyrus.

Heracles smiled and willingly took the proffered papyrus. He could really get used to this.

Once his newfound fans had been taken care of, Heracles went to King Minos' palace for an audience. As the son of Zeus and the seduced human woman Europa, King Minos was a result of another one of Zeus' conquests, just like Heracles, so they were in fact related. Heracles really hoped that meant he might get him some brownie points, and maybe the King would be receptive to him.

He met the king and dipped a gracious bow.

'Step-brother,' he began. He briefly wondered if that was a bit too forward, but King Minos showed no response to it. 'I'm performing labours for King

Eurystheus, and for this one I need to take your Cretan Bull back to him, if that's okay with you?'

'Oh, you're welcome to it,' the King replied, waving a hand. 'Nothing but trouble, that thing. It's not enough it has to destroy everything in sight but to father half-human, half-bull offspring with my wife is just *embarrassing*.'

'You know the bull well; can you help me?' Heracles wondered, trying to cash in any potential step-brotherly love.

King Minos snorted with laughter. 'What, the mighty Heracles, he who has slain the Nemean Lion and the Lernean Hydra, captured the Hind of Artemis and the Erymanthian Boar, dispersed the man-eating Stymphalian Birds and cleaned up a large amount of poo needs help to capture a pretty bull?'

'So ... that's a yes?' Heracles asked, confused.

Clearly King Minos wasn't feeling the family love as he scoffed, 'That was not a yes, you silly man,' he replied. 'Go and do it yourself, Hercules.'

Heracles sighed. 'Heracles,' he corrected.

'Whatever.'

'Thanks, step-brother, you've been really helpful,' Heracles said without conviction, and rapidly left the King's presence.

Heracles located the Cretan Bull wandering in a field near to Crete, leaving a trail of destruction in its wake. It really was magnificent, with perfect horns that were sharp and strong, a great, mighty neck, and powerful legs. Before Heracles could think of what to do, the bull spotted him.

It immediately snorted and began to stamp one of its front hooves, its head bobbing up and down, the sure signs of an impending charge. Heracles braced himself, and seconds later the bull charged, its head lowered to direct those pointy, thick horns straight at him.

Heracles threw out his arms, and as the bull met him, he caught its horns and brought it stumbling to a halt. They were too sturdy to snap, but with his now familiar and very useful demi-god strength, he strained to haul its head down, pushing the points of the horns away from himself. The bull roared, stamping its hoof and fighting back with startling strength. With all of the power he had in him, Heracles twisted the bull's head such a way that the bull let out a stressed bellow, and quickly began to relent. Within a matter of seconds, Heracles had control of the beast, and was able to sap its strength until the bull ceased its fight. Heracles mounted the fully subdued bull, and decided he'd ride it all the way back. That'd look impressive.

His increasing fanbase watched him as he rode, all of them shocked by his apparent taming of the wild and destructive creature that had plagued them for so long. He waved to his clapping and cheering audiences as he passed through the towns to the sea that separated the island from Greece, leaving many fainting fans in his wake. He crossed the sea, riding the bull the entire way, and headed straight back to King Eurystheus, feeling very happy that there were only three labours left to go.

The Eighth Labour: Heracles must retrieve the mares of Diomedes

King Eurystheus still wasn't allowing Heracles to enter the city with the results of his labours, as he was terrified. Instead, the King had come to meet him outside the palace, although he remained firmly within the city walls, surrounded by an entourage of guards. As King Eurystheus watched him riding the Cretan Bull, he really didn't want to admit that he was now quite impressed by Heracles and the ease with which he was completing the labours. Heracles really was throwing discus out of the park. But although the king was becoming increasingly impressed, he was also becoming increasingly irritated by the fact that his cousin was now becoming a bona fide hero among the people. Thus he resorted to childish insults when Heracles reappeared riding the great and feared bull.

'Oh, look at stupid Heracles riding his stupid bull!' King Eurystheus said.

Heracles just stared at him. King Eurystheus was sure Heracles was looking down on him these days. He didn't like that.

'Set it free, then on to your next labour,' the King ordered quickly, keen to get Heracles cut down to size with his next impossible task. 'I want you to bring me the mares of Diomedes!'

Asking around the public baths, Heracles rapidly discovered that this labour was going to be somewhat more challenging than the breezy nature of the previous two. However, he was becoming popular these days. He was naturally attracting crowds, and even the gods had given him gifts. Athena had gifted him a robe, Haephaestus a club and a coat of mail, Poseidon gave him horses, Hermes had given him a sword, and Apollo had presented him with a new bow and arrows. Even Demeter had realised he still felt guilt for the massacre of the Centaurs, and had initiated the Lesser Mysteries – a ritual of purification, which, unbeknown to Heracles, would greatly benefit him in the future.

As he was now so popular amid people and gods alike, he decided he'd try and gather some volunteers to help him accomplish the next labour.

'For this labour, I'm going to Thrace,' he told a gathered crowd. 'I'm looking for volunteers to come with me.'

'What's the labour?' one of the crowd asked.

'I've gotta bring the mares of Diomedes back to King Eurystheus,' Heracles replied.

'I'll come!' one of the crowd said eagerly, stepping out.

'Me too!' another one said.

'Thank you,' Heracles said, smiling.

'Are we gonna be back by the weekend?' one of the woman asked.

'Who's Diomedes?' a boy wondered.

'Is that the guy whose dad put him in a stew to serve the gods and then he got resurrected?' one of the men wondered.

'Nah, that's Pelops,' another one said.

'Diomedes is the guy who chats with termites,' one told them all with confidence.

'Excuse me, but that's Melampus, and he died, like, forever ago,' another disagreed.

'Diomedes of Thrace is a savage, the demi-god son of the God of War, Ares, and Cyrene, the fierce huntress. He feeds his mares with human flesh,' Heracles supplied casually.

Immediately the building buzz of excitement in the crowd died a hasty death. A couple of people who had stepped forward so quickly subtly stepped back into the crowd, looking a bit awkward.

'So, who's coming?' Heracles asked brightly.

Despite the revelation, a few brave people joined Heracles in his journey to the land of the war-loving Bistonians, over which Diomedes ruled. Heracles was clearly becoming better at this labours lark, as he even had a plan formed by the time they got there.

They waited until nightfall, and then gathered around the stables. At Heracles' command, the group charged into battle, bursting through the stable doors to meet a small group of startled grooms who were looking after the horses. Together Heracles and his group fought them. Within two minutes the fight was over, and the grooms lay dead.

Once the stable was secure, the group turned their attentions to the legendary mares. They were large, powerful horses with coarse, long, thick manes. They were clad in iron chains due to their overwhelming strength. They'd barely flinched at the bloodshed that had occurred in front of them, and even looked quite interested in the potential meal, eyeing the corpses of their ex-grooms strewn over the stables.

'What magnificent beasts!' Heracles' favourite companion, a boy named Abderus, said.

'Don't get too close! They'll eat you!' another man said. Heracles was sure that guy had regretted coming ever since they'd boarded the ship.

'What do we do now, Heracles?' another man asked.

'Drive them back to the sea,' Heracles said. 'So, if everyone could take one mare each ...'

No one moved, staring at the blooded lips of the man-eating horses and their stalls, filled with the remains of their lunch. One let out a loud neigh, opening its jaw to expose some indescribable bits of whoever had been the previous meal as it stomped its hoof on the ground. Several of the crowd jumped in alarm.

'Okay, okay, I'll take them,' Heracles conceded, and stepped forward.

Heracles drove the mares to the sea, followed by the rest of his group, who were standing just slightly out of reach of the man-eating beasts. However, as soon as they reached the sea, there came a distant battle cry of the incoming forces of the angered Bistonians.

'What was that?' one of the group asked in alarm, readying their weapons.

'I think Diomedes noticed,' Abderus answered, panicked. 'He's coming!'

Heracles made to ready for battle, but realised abruptly that he was still holding the mares. 'Err, can someone take these man-eating horses from me for a second?'

Once again, everyone subtly stepped back – all except Abderus, who looked at them all, sighed, and boldly came forward. 'I will,' he said.

'Thank you,' Heracles said, and handed them over. The boy was clearly trying everything in his power to look nonchalant. The mares immediately began to fight his hold. 'Abderus, you're brave,' he told the boy. 'Everyone else, with me!'

He led his group into the night, directly towards the horde of savages. Coming out of the gloom towards them, the Bistonians looked like the stuff of nightmares. They were all painted with blood and had black tattooed eyes. It was utterly terrifying.

Heracles sensed his group's hesitation at the sight. He brought them to a stop, and the Bistonians stopped too, the groups just twenty metres apart.

Emerging from the gloom and the horde, Diomedes of Thrace appeared, the bloodiest and most frightening of them all. He strolled towards Heracles with purpose. Heracles almost took his club in hand for defence against the attack he sensed coming, but stopped as Diomedes halted ten metres from him.

'You dare to steal my mares?' Diomedes of Thrace rasped, his voice petrifying.

'I'm completing labours for King Eurystheus,' Heracles stated boldly. 'You got a problem, take it up with him.'

'*You* are the one taking my mares,' Diomedes grated. 'Therefore, *you* shall suffer.'

'Look, as I explained,' Heracles began again, 'something happened, where I accidentally killed my wife and children, so I had to go to King Eurystheus to repent, and he –'

'Cease your prattle,' Diomedes interrupted, his black eyes seemingly on fire. 'You like my mares so much? *You can be fed to them!*'

Diomedes threw up his arm, and immediately his savages ran forward in a cacophony of fearsome battle cries. Heracles' group were suddenly fighting for their lives as the followers of Ares charged them without fear or hesitation.

Every person's fear caused them to fight bravely, battering the Bistonians with everything they had. Heracles himself made a beeline straight to Diomedes, engaging the god-born leader in fierce combat. Diomedes' strength rivalled Heracles', and the fight was bitter and long. After what felt like hours, Diomedes finally lay dead. At the death of Diomedes, the remaining Bistonians fled. Heracles quickly checked his companions. Some were injured, but no one was dead. Despite their wounds, they cheered in victory, and Heracles smiled.

As they returned to Abderus and the mares, it became clear that something quite horrific had happened in their absence. The mares were happily chewing something, blood was on the ground, and the boy was nowhere to be seen.

'Oh, by all the deities!' one of Heracles' group curse, shocked. 'They ate him!'

Heracles dropped to his knees, feeling as though he'd been struck with a javelin. He couldn't believe it. He cursed himself for leaving Abderus with the mares, when he'd clearly not been in control of them. The young, brave boy he'd come to love was dead, and it was all his fault.

Heracles wept.

'We'll bury Abderus,' Heracles decided after a few moments, wiping away his tears with his lionskin as he straightened up. 'Then, I'll found a city by his grave, and name it in his honour. The city of Abdera.'

Heracles took the mares back to King Eurystheus, who steeled himself enough to go beyond his kingdom with an entourage to release the mares into the wild.

'Be free!' King Eurystheus declared, smiling broadly. 'Roam these lands and be the magnificent creatures you are, striding so boldly with your great manes and your great power of stead!'

And indeed, the mares roamed, free and wild, eventually coming to the base of Mount Olympus, where they were promptly eaten by wild beasts.

The deities Pan and Artemis watched the mares being eaten, wincing at the sight.

'This ain't right, man,' Pan said.

'So not only have we now got the Erymanthian Boar in completely the wrong place, we've also got the Cretan Bull wandering around Greece killing people, and the mares of Thrace are being eaten by beasts of Olympus ...' Artemis mused. 'These people are doing nothing for ecological balance.'

'Right on,' Pan agreed. 'It's so hairy, man.'

Artemis sighed. 'Heracles will be done soon. Right?'

The Ninth Labour: Heracles must fetch the Belt of Hippolyte

'Daddy ...' King Eurystheus' grown daughter began, smiling sweetly at her father as he sat on his throne, looking important.

'Yes, my little olive?' the King said, beaming at his daughter.

'You know you've got that guy doing those labours for you ...'

'Yes, my little chestnut?'

'There's something I *really* want ...'

'And what do you want, my little piece of leavened bread?'

'It's the Lesser Dionysia festival soon, and I've got a dress, but I don't have a matching accessory ...'

'What accessory would you like, my freshly-caught pike-fish?'

'Well ... I've always *really* wanted the Belt of Hippolyte ...' she said, fluttering her eyelashes at him.

He nodded, still smiling. 'Then of course you shall have it, my soft-boiled Egyptian Goose egg!'

'Thanks, Daddy!' his adult daughter replied, skipping out of the door. The King smiled for a moment, and then requested Heracles' presence. He was rather pleased. Admittedly, he'd been running out of labours, and nothing was too much for his adorable fragrant lentil soup.

Once again, Heracles gathered a group of comrades who were willing to embark on the journey to the Thermodon river, where the queen of the Amazons, Hippolyte, had her tribe. Fierce and highly capable warriors, the Amazons were exclusively female, and the tribe lived apart from men. Heracles knew of the belt which King Eurystheus desired – rumour had it the belt had been given to Hippolyte by the god Ares. Hippolyte wasn't likely to give up the belt easily. So he was pleasantly surprised when, soon after they'd arrived, Hippolyte herself came to meet them, without a hint of confrontation.

The journey had been long, arduous, and harsh as they sailed, their destination the port of Themiscyra. Tired and hungry, Heracles' group finally arrived, dragging their feet as they made their way off of the ship. To Heracles' complete surprise, they were met by Hippolyte. He readied for a fight, but Hippolyte didn't lay a hand on her weapons.

'You are Heracles?' Hippolyte asked.

Heracles nodded, still a little guarded, but more relaxed than he usually was in confrontations such as this. 'Yeah, that's me,' he said.

'I've been hearing of your labours. You're quite the hero, aren't you? From slaying the Nemean Lion and capturing the mares of Diomedes, your feats are known across this land.'

Heracles shrugged a little.

'Why have you come here?' Hippolyte asked.

'For my next labour, King Eurystheus has asked for your belt,' Heracles said, pointing at the belt Hippolyte was wearing around her chest, which was currently holding her sword and her spear.

'I see,' Hippolyte replied, looking down at the belt the God of War had gifted her. After a moment's thought, she nodded and smiled. 'Heracles, I have great respect for you and your strength. You shall have the belt you seek. I offer you no challenge for it, and I wish you only good fortune on your final labour.'

Heracles smiled in returned. 'Cheers,' he said, glancing back at his comrades, who all seemed fairly relieved that they weren't going to fight, yet somewhat slightly miffed by the anti-climax to their gruelling journey. Not that Heracles particularly cared – after he returned the belt to King Eurystheus, he only had one labour to go.

Hera watched Hippolyte and Heracles' conversation, becoming increasingly more infuriated with just how easily Heracles was going to finish this labour. These labours were meant to kill the little brat, not increase his friends list. The new fanbase Heracles had acquired in the wake of his labours was irritating enough, but to have the people involved in his labours willingly finishing them for him with no resistance? That was just the icing on Hera's angry cake.

No, Hera decided. She wasn't having this. Heracles didn't get to do this. This was supposed to be a death-defying labour. If Hippolyte wasn't going to make it a labour, then Hera had to intervene.

Hera vanished from her observation spot and reappeared in the Amazon stronghold where Hippolyte's army was gathered. She changed her form into that of an Amazon, and without a moment's hesitation, jogged straight up to the nearest Amazon.

'Queen Hippolyte is with strangers at Themiscyra! They're going to take her!'

'What!?' the Amazon warrior gasped. 'We must save our Queen!'

Hera let out a rousing battle cry and ran to the next nearest Amazon. 'Strangers are here to take our Queen!'

'No way!' the Amazon said, stunned.

Hera continued all around the stronghold, repeating her lie to make sure every Amazon knew. Within a few minutes, all of the Amazons were in their battle armour and mounting horses. With screams of rage, the Amazons charged out of the camp, riding to the port.

Job done, Hera smiled her unpleasant best, and vanished to watch events play out to their surely bloody conclusion.

Hippolyte was just unfastening the belt to give to Heracles when suddenly there came the din of loud and furious Amazon battle cries. Startled, everyone looked up and saw Hippolyte's army charging towards them on horseback with their weapons drawn.

'It's a trick!' one of Heracles' group yelled.

Before Hippolyte could protest, Heracles' survival instinct kicked in. He grabbed the stunned Hippolyte and killed her on the spot. As her lifeless body slumped to the ground, Heracles grabbed the belt.

'Run!' he cried to his friends, but it was too late. The Amazons reached them, and once again it was a bitter fight to the death.

Hera was transfixed by the sight of the fearsome, bloody battle. She watched, her irritation once again rising rapidly as Heracles fought his way through the mass of highly-skilled Amazon warriors without too much trouble. He and his remaining companions then boarded their ship, leaving the piles of dead Amazons where they'd fallen.

'Will *nothing* kill this little twerp!?' Hera cried.

THE TENTH LABOUR: HERACLES MUST RETRIEVE THE CATTLE OF GERYON

'You took your time,' King Eurystheus said as Heracles finally delivered Hippolyte's Belt to him. 'I thought you were finally dead.'

'Sorry,' Heracles said, shrugging slightly. 'Had to stop over in Troy and save it from pestilence and a sea monster.'

'Do I look like I care?' the king said, unimpressed. 'You were so late that my daughter had to go to the Lesser Dionysia festival without an accessory!'

'Tragic,' Heracles muttered insincerely.

'Pardon?'

'Yeah, sorry,' Heracles said loudly, and moved on. 'What's my tenth labour?'

King Eurystheus smiled, self-satisfied. He'd clearly been thinking about this one for a while. 'For this labour, you must travel to the end of the world, and bring me the cattle of the monster Geryon!'

Heracles was feeling quite chirpy as he embarked on the labour, safe in the knowledge that once it was completed, he would have fully repented for the murder of his family.

He knew of the monster Geryon. Geryon was the grandson of Medusa, the dangerous gorgon with snakes for hair that immediately turned anyone who looked at her to stone. He was also the grandson of two Titans, primordial gods of great power and reputation. As such, Geryon was rumoured to be quite a sight to behold. He was said to be three men joined together at the waist, with three heads, and some had even claimed he had wings. He was also a giant, and kept a two-headed hound named Orthus that was rumoured to be the sibling of Cerberus, the three-headed Hound guarding the underworld. In fact, Orthus was the father of the Nemean Lion. Heracles was under no illusions – his final labour wasn't going to be easy.

He travelled the lands for many weeks, challenged only by the wild beasts of the continent, which he killed without much trouble. As he reached the passage between modern day Spain and Morocco, he decided that after such a long journey, and as a symbol of his labours, he would leave his mark. With a mighty blow, he split the mountain that sat between the two modern continents of Europe and Africa, creating a strait between them. He stood back to admire his work. The Pillars of Heracles, he decided they'd be named.

He resumed his journey. He had to sail to the isle of Erythia, where the monster Geryon had his home. As he pondered on how to cross the sea, the unrelenting scorching heat of the sun bore down on the hero. Heracles sat there, becoming increasingly agitated, until he finally lost his temper.

'Stop being so hot!' he yelled, and promptly fired an arrow at the sun.

'HEY, *WHAT* DO YOU THINK YOU'RE DOING?' a voice boomed from what seemed to be somewhere in the sky.

Heracles looked around, shocked, as he readied his club for a fight. 'Who's there!?'

'WHO DO YOU THINK, *MORON?*' the voice responded. 'HERE I AM, JUST RIDING MY CHARIOT ACROSS THE SKY TO GIVE

MANKIND THE SUNRISE AND SUNSET EACH DAY, AND YOU GO AND FIRE AN **ARROW** AT ME! WHAT'S YOUR *PROBLEM!?*'

Ah, it was Helios, the Titan-god of the sun, Heracles realised. 'You're too hot!' Heracles complained. 'I can't think with this stupid amount of heat!'

'WELL, I'M *SORRY,*' Helios replied sarcastically. 'YOU PEOPLE NEED TO **SERIOUSLY** SORT OUT WHAT YOU WANT! ONE DAY YOU'RE LIKE, "IT'S JULY, I'M COLD, WHERE'S HELIOS?" THEN NEXT MINUTE YOU'RE LIKE, "THIS IS WAY TOO HOT! I WANT BOREOS! STOP IT, HELIOS!" MAKE UP YOUR *MINDS!*'

Heracles sighed, lowering his bow. It wasn't worth it to argue about heat with the Sun, he mused. 'Look, I'm sorry,' he told Helios. 'I get annoyed when I'm hot.'

'WHO FIRES AN *ARROW* AT THE SUN WHEN THEY'RE HOT, ANYWAY?' Helios said. 'YOU MUST BE **STUPID!**'

Heracles fell silent, scuffing his sandals on the dirt, ashamed.

Helios sighed. 'LOOK, I'M SORRY, ERR ... WHAT'S YOUR NAME?'

'Heracles,' Heracles replied.

There was a brief pause. 'OH, I KNOW YOU, YOU'RE DOING THOSE LABOURS! I'VE BEEN WATCHING YOU. VERY IMPRESSIVE.'

'Thanks.'

'WHAT ARE YOU DOING ALL THE WAY OVER HERE AT THE END OF THE WORLD?'

'I'm trying to get to the Isle of Erythia,' Heracles replied.

There was another pause as Helios was clearly looking at him. 'HOW ARE YOU GOING TO GET TO THE ISLE WITHOUT A BOAT?'

'That's what I was wondering,' Heracles said.

'OH, YOU'RE MAKING ME FEEL BAD,' Helios admitted coyly. 'LOOK, HERCULES ...'

'Heracles,' Heracles corrected.

'WHATEVER. ALTHOUGH FIRING AN ARROW AT ME WAS DUMB, I'VE GOT TO ADMIT, I LIKE YOUR PLUCK. I'M IMPRESSED THAT ARROW EVEN REACHED ME. YOU'RE AN ALL RIGHT GUY, HERACLES. I LIKE THE

CUT OF YOUR JIB. I'M GOING TO HELP YOU OUT. I'LL GIVE YOU MY CUP, SO YOU CAN CROSS THE SEA TO ERYTHIA.'

Heracles was confused. 'How am I going to ride across the sea in a cup?'

'IT'S QUITE A LARGE CUP,' Helios assured him. 'GOOD LUCK WITH YOUR WHOLE LABOURS THING.'

Helios' cup *was* quite large, and entirely made of gold. Heracles happily made his way across the sea to the isle where the monster Geryon dwelt. He alighted, finding himself in a beautiful place that was bathed in the red light of Helios' sunset. There was a small mountain, so Heracles lodged there to get some rest.

Heracles was woken up by the sound of grunts and sniffing. He knew immediately what it was – the legendary two-headed dog, Orthus, come to kill him.

Making as little noise as possible, Heracles got up and moved into cover, clutching his club. Seconds later the dog came into view, and immediately spotted him hiding among the bushes.

It rushed at him, its terrible fangs and sharp claws in a frenzy, trying to kill him. Heracles, as ever, swung his club with precision and promptly bludgeoned the terrifying hound to death.

Heracles rose from his hiding place, but had to duck when he heard a voice nearby.

'Come bye, lad! Come bye!'

It was Eurytion, the herdsman, Heracles realised. He readied himself once again, the club still in his grip. Eurytion appeared among the flora, calling for the hound.

'That'll do, boy! That'll ... agh!'

The herdsman cried out as Heracles launched forward and swung his club to connect with Eurytion's head. The herdsman died immediately.

Without the herdsman or the guard dog, rustling the cattle was going to be a lot easier, Heracles realised. He had to make his move, now.

He gathered his belongings, and headed to the pastures.

The underworld daemon and part-time cattle herder of Hades, Menoetes, had watched as Heracles had slain the hound and the herdsman, and immediately scuttled to Geryon to inform him of the events.

'Heracles is here to steal your cattle,' the daemon rasped. 'He is heading towards the pastures now.'

'How dare he!' Geryon said, all three of his heads looking very annoyed. 'I shall smite this Heracles where he stands!'

Arming himself with his best weapons, the fearsome monster Geryon immediately left to kill Heracles.

Heracles was just musing on how unlaborious this labour was when Geryon finally made an appearance. Heracles had already been driving the cattle back to Helios' cup when the monster arrived in all his gory glory. Heracles realised that all the stories about the monster's gruesome appearance had been true. Even Heracles was quite unsettled by the sight of Geryon scuttling towards him, weapons already drawn.

'Hey,' Heracles greeted, but clearly Geryon wasn't in the mood for conversation. He took one look at what Heracles was doing and immediately launched into battle. They struggled momentarily before Hercules shot an arrow covered in the Lernean Hydra's blood, which killed Geryon immediately.

This final labour still wasn't that laborious, Heracles mused, as he drove the cattle onto Helios' cup and sailed back across the strait.

By the time Heracles got back to King Eurystheus, he was utterly exhausted.

It had turned out that stealing the cattle from the ferocious three-bodied legendary monster had been the easy part. After returning the cup to Helios his luck had turned very sour. At Liguria, the sons of Poseidon had tried to steal the cattle, both of whom Heracles had to kill. Shortly after that at Rhegium, a bull had broken free and swam across the sea to Sicily, where another son of Poseidon, Eryx, had taken it as part of his herd. Heracles had had to kill him too, in a wrestling bout. After that, Hera had caused the cattle to run amok, and Heracles had spent a fair amount of time trying to round them up again. Heracles, oblivious to Hera's interference and very annoyed by these tedious delays in completing his labours, blamed the river Strymon and filled it with rocks to make it unnavigable. Admittedly, that meant his journey had taken even longer, but he felt better for it.

Still, as he finally reached King Eurystheus with the herd, he was very pleased. He'd completed his ten labours. He proudly presented them to the King, who nodded approvingly.

'Excellent work, Heracles,' King Eurystheus said happily. 'I shall sacrifice these to Hera.'

'Sure,' Heracles replied, not really caring. 'Well, that's me done here, nice seeing you and all that, but ...'

'Where do you think you're going?' the King asked, bewildered.

Heracles frowned. 'Um, ten labours, right? That was the deal. I'm done.'

'Excuse me,' the King said, looking smug. 'I think you'll find you owe me two labours, actually.'

Heracles stared at him for a moment, before he suddenly laughed. 'Oh! Good joke!' he said happily.

'No joke,' the King insisted, utterly deadpan.

Heracles was really starting to get worried now. 'Um ... but it was ten labours. They're done. I'm going, now.'

'You, Heracles, owe me two labours.'

'... No, I don't?'

'I'm sorry, but you haven't played by the rules, Heracles,' the King said smugly. 'On your second labour you had help to kill the hydra, and on your fifth labour you tried to ask for payment. Therefore, those two labours don't count.'

'Are you serious?'

'Completely serious.'

'But ...'

'Therefore, for your eleventh labour, you –'

'But this isn't fair!' Heracles interrupted. 'You made those rules up after I got back!'

'No, I didn't.'

'Yes, you did!'

'No, I didn't.'

Heracles sighed. He wasn't going to get anywhere with this. He even momentarily mused on the fact that he'd enlisted help on more than one occasion, and quickly decided not to say anything about it, else he'd be doing these labours forever. After all, it had already been eight years. 'Okay, okay. What do you want me to do?' he asked, keen to get on with it.

'You must fetch me the apples of the Hesperides!' the King declared, delighted.

With a sigh, Heracles left.

The Eleventh Labour: Heracles must fetch the Apples of the Hesperides

Heracles knew very little about the Hesperides, and in fact had no idea where he was even going. He ended up boarding a boat, and was glad to meet a young and eager bard. The young bard, wanting desperately to try out his new lyre, was keen to please, and he composed a song on the spot when Heracles asked him about the Hesperides.

'I sing of the Golden Apples,' the bard began, plucking his lyre:

'When Zeus took Hera as his wife, the Earth gave apples with eternal life.

'Nymphs of the evening, numbered three, or four or seven, don't ask me!

'They are the Hespirides, daughters of Nyx, who guard these apples so nobody picks.

'Not trusting them, Hera placed Lardon, a fearsome dragon, in the garden!

'The dragon has one hundred heads, and he's immortal so you'll be dead.

'With each face the voices change, I hear he's got a vocal range.

'The garden's place is known to none, seriously, you're trying? Good luck and have fun.'

The bard beamed as he finished, looking at Heracles. 'How was that?'

'Um, okay,' Heracles replied, not wanting to discourage the eager young bard.

'Why, thank you,' the bard said, beaming. 'That was my first performance!'

'So, no one knows where this garden is?' Heracles asked, trying to change the subject.

The bard shook his head. 'Maybe the Old Man of the Sea, you know, Nereus? He knows things.'

'Where can I find him?'

'Illyria – try asking the nymphs at the river Eridanus.'

'Ah, cool. Thanks.'

'You're welcome,' the bard replied, and then suddenly looked delighted. 'Hey! I could come with you! I could get some great material for my songs!'

Heracles frowned a little. 'It's gonna be dangerous,' he warned the young bard.

'That's okay!' the bard assured him. 'You can't write a good song without nearly being killed. That's what my dad used to say, just before he got trampled by those horses.'

'Okay,' Heracles said, nodding.

Following the bard's advice, Heracles and the bard journeyed towards Illyria, Heracles telling the bard all about his labours of the past eight years to pass the time. Halfway there, they were just crossing a river when suddenly there was a shout.

'Heracles!' a man yelled. 'I challenge you to single combat!'

Heracles sighed. 'Can we do this later? I'm kind of busy.'

'You're rejecting my challenge?' the man asked, and stepped into view. Heracles knew him. This was Cycnus, the son of the God of War, Ares. He was large, strong, and clearly very eager to battle, his teeth gritted and his face set. 'You've killed my brother and my sister, and I will in turn kill you!'

Heracles frowned. 'Really? Who were they?'

'Diomedes of Thrace and Hippolyte!' Cycnus yelled.

Heracles realised the unfortunate family connection. Diomedes had been the crazy man with the man-eating horses, and Hippolyte had been Queen of the Amazons. 'Look, I'm sorry,' Heracles started, hands in the air. 'But Diomedes kinda asked for it, and Hippolyte was a complete misunderstanding. I swear none of it was my fault.'

Cycnus ignored that. 'Do you accept my challenge!?'

Heracles sighed. He wasn't going to get out of this. 'Right, okay. Sure,' he said, and readied his weapon as the bard, stunned into silence, quickly dived behind a tree with a high-pitched squeak of fear.

The two demi-gods came together in a whirl of ferocity. What Heracles hadn't anticipated was the appearance of Ares, who started throwing fireballs at the hero in support of his son. Despite the clear handicap, Heracles triumphed, and killed yet another of Ares' children.

Enraged, Ares immediately appeared in front of him, where his son lay dead.

'You will *die* Heracles!' Ares screamed ferociously, and immediately launched a godly assault. Heracles struggled badly to contend with the god's power, and for the first time in his life, knew that this wasn't a battle he was going to win.

Having been constantly blasted by Ares' fire, he fell, utterly exhausted, to the ground. Triumphantly, Ares stood over him, raising his hand for the killing blast, when suddenly a huge thunderbolt struck between the two combatants. Both of them were sent flying backwards as the land around them burned with fire and rippled with electricity.

'I WOULDN'T DO THAT IF I WERE YOU, ARES,' Zeus boomed.

'THIS HAS *NOTHING* TO DO WITH YOU, DAD!' Ares yelled.

'YOU **WILL NOT** KILL YOUR BROTHER!' Zeus replied.

'HE'S KILLED *THREE* OF MY CHILDREN!' Ares screamed.

'WELL, TOUGH TURNIPS! MOVE ALONG, ARES!'

'THIS ISN'T *FAIR!* YOU DON'T UNDERSTAND ME!'

'I'LL HAVE NONE OF YOUR LIP, YOUNG MAN!'

Ares harrumphed, and disappeared.

Heracles and the bard traversed the lands, on a quest to find the Garden of the Hesperides. Eventually they arrived at Libya, and Helios was again on hand to lend Heracles his cup for their journey across the sea. They eventually arrived at Mount Caucasus, where they decided to have a rest.

Heracles, confused by the intermittent yells of pain coming from the mountain, asked the bard what was going on.

'You don't know about Prometheus?' the bard asked.

'Um, no?' Heracles said.

The bard smiled. 'I've got a song for that! It's a cover song, though,' he muttered, obviously annoyed he hadn't written something he was about to sing. He then launched into a cheerful tune about Prometheus stealing fire from the gods to give to men, and his terrible fate of having an eagle feed on his liver for eternity.

'My dad did that?' Heracles mused, scratching his beard.

The bard shrugged. 'That's what they say happened.'

Another cry of pain echoed from the mountain into the valley they were.

'I don't think that's fair,' Heracles mused.

The bard had obviously been hanging around with him long enough to know what Heracles was thinking. 'You're not seriously going to do something about this, are you?' he asked. 'It's by order of Zeus.'

Heracles shrugged nonchalantly, and immediately headed up the mountain.

Heracles arrived as the helpless and tortured Titan was being pecked by an atrociously large eagle. With the eagle clearly distracted by its meal, Heracles took an advantageous position, readied his bow, and aimed an arrow at the bird.

The arrow cut through the air and slammed into the eagle. Hugely surprised, the eagle squawked and, two seconds later, fell to the ground in a plume of feathers.

Heracles stepped out from cover as Prometheus looked around, astonished. Their eyes met.

'You! Did you just kill that eagle?' Prometheus asked.

Heracles slicked back his hair. 'Yeah, I guess I did,' he said, and with a few mighty blows against the chains, he freed Prometheus.

Prometheus sat up, still very shocked. 'Who are you?'

The eager bard jumped out of the bushes, smiling broadly. 'I've got a song for that!' he said.

Heracles shrugged and gestured for the bard to fill in the required exposition.

'I sing of Heracles!' the bard started:

'He must perform what Eurystheus asks, by completing twelve impossible tasks,

'Many monsters he has killed, and now ten labours are fulfilled,

'So when the King wanted some apples, off went Heracles on his travels,

'Cycnus challenged him with hate, for his siblings' deathly fate,

'Cycnus died and Ares got mad, fighting til he was saved by his dad!

'He travelled on to the Old Man of the Sea, helped by some nymphs who knew of his deeds.

'Heracles jumped into the waters, where Nereus lived with fifty daughters.

'Wise and prophetic and seaweeds for hair, he was fast asleep when our hero got there!

'Heracles bound him and asked for directions, but Nereus, of course, he had his objections!

'He morphed into objects including some bread, 'til finally it just had to be said:

'He told Heracles the way to go, and our hero went on to continue the show!

'But whilst in Libya – it wasn't his fault – Poseidon's son, Antaeous, made him halt.

'Antaeous wrestled and posed a threat, but our hero didn't break a sweat!

'Antaeous' power came from the ground, so Heracles lifted him up abound!

'He hugged him tight until Antaeous broke, causing the son to choke with a croak!

'Heracles went to the Egyptian lands, but he was abducted by evil hands!

'Egypt had been in the grip of a famine; but alas, it was not just salmon!

'Every year a stranger was killed, as a sacrifice to be fulfilled.

'So they wanted our hero to kill for Zeus, but Heracles didn't, and he broke loose!

'Being annoyed with everyone, he killed the ruler and his son!

'Now he's here to save you today, Heracles, the hero, bravo, I'd say!'

'Thanks for that,' Prometheus said to the bard, pulling a face. 'So, what, you're Zeus' son?'

Heracles nodded.

'There's a turn up for the tomes,' Prometheus muttered. 'I've been here for thirty years. I never thought I'd be free. I guess I owe you, Heracles. What did you say you were looking for?'

'Our hero must find the apples of gold, kept in a garden that –'

'The Apples of the Hespirides?' Prometheus interrupted.

'Yeah,' Heracles replied, nodding.

'I might be able to help you, there.'

'What are you going to do about this?' Heracles asked, gesturing to the rock and the dead eagle.

'Oh, I'll find someone gullible to take my place. Zeus won't even notice,' Prometheus replied, standing up. 'Right, these apples. Do you know my brother, Atlas?'

'The one who holds the Heavens on his shoulders?' Heracles remembered that from some school lesson.

'Yeah, him. It's gonna pain me to have you do this to him, but I owe you. If you want these apples, you'll need to trick Atlas.'

'How's that going to help?' Heracles wondered.

'The Hespirides are his daughters,' Prometheus explained. 'He can get the apples for you, but you need to do *exactly* as I tell you.'

'Okay,' Heracles affirmed.

Following Prometheus' plan, Heracles went to the land of the Hyperboreans to visit Atlas. For his part in the War against the ruler of the Gods, the Titan God had been condemned by Zeus to hold up the Heavens for an eternity.

He felt a bit sorry for the Titan when he saw him. Atlas was clearly exhausted and pained by his difficult eternal labour, once again imposed by Heracles' own father. Heracles felt a bit bad for what he was about to do.

'Atlas,' Heracles greeted the Titan.

'Um, hello!' the Titan moaned from the strain of holding the heavens. 'Who are you?'

The bard immediately launched into song with delight. 'Heracles, the strong and the brave, has come to scam you for –'

'Shut up!' Heracles hissed to the bard.

'Oh, sorry,' the bard said as he realised he'd nearly given the game away, quickly putting his lyre behind his back.

'I'm Heracles,' Heracles said to the Titan, hoping he hadn't noticed. 'I think you can help me.'

'I can't help anyone,' the Titan complained. 'I've got to hold up the Heavens for an eternity, and it's bloody tiring, you know!'

'I really need to get the Apples of the Hesperides for King Eurystheus.'

'You want the golden apples from my daughters' garden?' Atlas moaned out. 'Not a chance. There's a hundred-headed immortal dragon, and those girls could skin the Nemean Lion alive.'

'I think we can help each other out,' Heracles said, copying what Prometheus had said word for word. 'I want the apples, and you want to stop holding up the Heavens, don't you?'

Atlas looked at him, clearly intrigued. 'Go on.'

'If you get me the apples, I'll take your place.'

Atlas frowned. 'Really?'

'Yes,' Heracles said, nodding.

'Deal,' Atlas said, clearly too eager to get the Heavens off his shoulders to stop and think about what Heracles was doing. They traded places, and suddenly Heracles was straining under the weight of the Heavens. He hadn't quite anticipated just how heavy the Heavens were, despite the clue being in the name. Even with the usually unyielding strength that had carried him through ten labours, Heracles was struggling very, very badly.

'Oh, that's a relief,' Atlas breathed, laughing a little with joy. 'Talk about taking a weight off your shoulders! Oh, thanks so much for this. I'll go and get those apples for you.'

Atlas left to fulfil his side of the bargain, leaving Heracles standing there, pained and immobile, with only the bard to keep him company. The plan was on track, and everything had happened exactly as Prometheus had said.

When Atlas returned holding the golden apples, Heracles was seriously beginning to falter. Atlas noticed that, and smiled reassuringly.

'Honest, it gets a bit easier after the tenth year,' Atlas told him. 'Thirtieth year's the hardest, though.'

'Yeah,' Heracles managed in a groan.

'I've got the apples. Don't worry, I'll take them to the King for you,' Atlas said. 'Thanks Heracles, you're a pal.'

'That's okay,' Heracles managed, and returned to trying to recall Prometheus' words. 'Hey, before you leave, could you do me one last thing?'

'Sure, friend, anything,' Atlas replied.

'My head's hurting from the weight,' Heracles complained. 'Can you take the Heavens for a bit while I put a pillow on it?'

'Really?' Atlas moaned. 'I thought you were holding them now.'

'Please,' Heracles begged.

'Ah, all right, then,' Atlas said with a sigh, and took the weight back, his pained expression immediately returning. Heracles paused, gazing at him, before picking up the apples.

Atlas looked horrified. 'No, what are you doing? We had a deal!'

'I'm sorry,' Heracles said genuinely. He walked away, his bard in tow.

'I thought we were friends!' Atlas yelled. 'Heracles, come back!'

Not saying a word, Heracles continued until Atlas was out of sight.

'HERACLES!' the Titan yelled desperately.

Heracles sighed. One day he should do something for Atlas. Maybe he could build some pillars to holding up the skies for him, he mused, as he made his way back to King Eurystheus.

The Twelfth Labour: Heracles must retrieve Cerberus

King Eurystheus sighed loudly as he absently stirred his wine with his finger, having to endure the increasing frustration of his cousin's apparent knack for being magnificent as Heracles arrived back with the golden apples. Heracles had now performed eleven impossible labours seemingly without much problem – he'd killed and captured legendary animals and gone up against Gods and Goddesses whilst traversing the world. The King's own people now referred to Heracles as a Hero, while King Eurystheus had been sitting here eating grapes.

No, he decided. It was now time for the final labour. He had to think of something truly impossible, something that would *surely* kill Zeus' son once and for all.

As Heracles stood there waiting to hear of his final labour, a blinder of an idea hit the King right between the eyes. Something truly impossible. Something not even a demi-God could accomplish. Something that, reasonably, would kill his cousin.

He straightened up in his throne, trying to look important. 'For your final labour, you will capture and fetch me, alive, Cerberus!'

The entire room stilled and fell quiet with shock.

'Oh, Zeus,' the bard blasphemed, wide-eyed. 'That's the guardian beast of the Underworld!'

King Eurystheus tried not to smirk. 'Indeed, it is.'

'Are you sure?' Heracles asked, stupefied.

The King was very pleased to see Heracles, finally, a little nervous. 'Get going,' he encouraged.

Heracles and his tagalong bard stepped out into the city, where it was raining, musing on the sheer enormity of the labour that lay ahead. Heracles may have killed Cerberus' siblings, Orthus and the Lernean Hydra, as well as Orthus' child, the Nemean Lion, but Cerberus was an entirely different matter. It had been picked to guard the Underworld for a reason. Everyone knew of it. Not only that, but to get to Cerberus he'd have to descend into the Underworld, the realm of Hades, a journey from which no mortal had ever returned. The realm of the dead was a place of pure mystery, its secrets unknown, and the stories of those who had met it usually ended in death. The King clearly had no intention of ever seeing Heracles again.

'So, um, what's the plan?' the bard wondered, sounding quite scared.

Heracles, who had grown from his beginnings as a plan-less idiot to someone who consistently made quite good plans, was completely at a loss over what he was going to do, or even where he was going to start. 'I don't know,' he confessed.

The bard cleared his throat nervously, and made a vague gesture over his shoulder to indicate he was leaving. 'You know what? I'll head off now. I think I've got enough material for a lifetime.'

'But you can't go, you ...'

'I know, I know, I don't want to leave either, but err ... err ...' the bard stumbled, clearly trying to make something up. 'My brother's, um, taking part in the chariot race, and I should really go and support him!'

'Okay,' Heracles replied, sighing.

'Don't worry; whatever happens, I'll always sing songs of you!' the bard assured him.

'Thank you.'

'I'll give you one last tune!' the bard said, smiling inanely, and his whipped out his trusty lyre before Heracles could stop him.

'The Hound of Hades is quite a sight, the dragon in its tail's a fright.

'Snakes for a mane, you'd be insane, to challenge this beast without a priest.

'It's lion's claws are oh so sharp, sharper than a broken harp,

'Yet still he went on to fetch it from, the depths of hell where dead souls dwell.

'He'll probably die so I should say, to you on this rainy day,

'Heracles fought, but he was caught, in its claws and its jaws.

'Such a shame that he's dead now, but he will always be my pal!'

And with that rousing chorus that showed a complete lack of faith in the demi-God, the bard left.

Heracles, after some deliberation, decided he needed to prepare himself. He went to Eleusis to meet a priest, who was said to be a part of the Eleusinian Mysteries – a cult of the Goddesses Demeter and Persephone, who were known for their connections to the Underworld. If anyone knew how Heracles could descend to and ascend from the Underworld it would surely be this cult.

After he'd arrived, he rapidly discovered that being initiated into the Eleusinian Mysteries required more than just willingness. To be a part of their cult, he had to join the Greater Mysteries, and for that, he had to be purified. Demeter's motivations in creating the Lesser Mysteries just before Heracles had captured the mares of Diomedes became clear. Heracles eagerly took part in the Lesser Mysteries, and was purified of the killing of the centaurs, which allowed him to sign up.

After his initiation, he sought an entrance to the Underworld, and chose Taenarum, a well-known gateway to Hades for those willing to enter. Heracles was hardly willing, but he was determined to complete this final labour. He entered the gateway.

Heracles had always prided himself on being unfazed by most things, but as he descended into the dark and murky depths of Hades, he became more and more unsettled. He could hear the distant screams of the tortured dead, mixed with the smell of rot, and the only light came from flicking fires around him.

He reached the river that had to be crossed to get to the gates of Hades, where he came across a group of dead souls, only half-visible in their dead forms, standing on the bank, waiting to be taken across the water by Charon, the ferryman of Hades. His appearance was nothing short of terrifying. He looked like an old, ugly Athenian seaman who'd long since died – his skin white, his cheeks sunken, and his eyes seemingly on fire.

Heracles decided to stay back a moment as Charon's boat arrived at the shore, ready to take more dead souls. One of the dead man stepped forward to board the boat.

'Coin,' Charon whispered, extending an emaciated hand to the dead man.

'I was buried without a coin in my mouth,' the man replied, scared.

'Then you shall not cross to Hades,' Chiron replied in a whisper.

'Please, no!' the man begged. 'I don't want to be standing on this riverbank for eternity!'

'There are only two rules to cross in my boat,' Charon breathed, staring at the dead man, 'you must be dead, and you must have a coin.'

Heracles subtly frisked himself. He wasn't dead, and neither did he have a coin. This wasn't good.

'Then I'll swim!' the man declared, pointing at the river.

'There are five rivers of Hades. The Acheron, known as the river of pain. The Styx, the river of hate. Cocytus, the river of lamentation. Phlegethon, the river of fire, and Lethe, the river of forgetfulness.' Charon pointed down to the river under his boat. 'Perhaps you would like to find out which one this is by diving into it.'

The dead man stepped back, shaking.

Heracles didn't know what he was going to do, but he got in line anyway. A few dead souls boarded the boat with their coins, and then it was Heracles' turn.

'Coin,' Charon whispered, holding out his hand.

'I haven't got a coin,' Heracles replied.

Charon gazed at him. 'You are also not dead.'

The dead people around him looked at Heracles, shocked.

'I'm Heracles, and I want to board this boat,' Heracles said strongly.

'You shall not,' Charon breathed.

Heracles stared at the weak-looking old demon, and decided he could take him. He grabbed Charon's ferryman's pole and promptly hit the demon with it.

Charon fell to the deck with a yelp and Heracles stepped aboard.

'Next stop, the Gates of Hades,' Heracles prompted the bewildered ferryman, giving him back his pole.

Charon glowered at him, but now he was on the boat, Charon couldn't get him off. Charon simply turned to his next dead soul to receive a coin for their passage.

The boat docked, and Heracles had continued onwards without hesitation. On the way to the Gates of Hades he met the Gorgon Medusa, whose hair, made of snakes, was known to turn people to stone. Heracles had immediately drawn his sword, but Hermes, who had gifted him the sword, had assured him she was no longer a threat since being killed by Perseus. He carried on, and the screams and shouts of those condemned to eternal suffering in Tartarus, the worst part of Hades, continued to ring out from somewhere below him.

Just a short distance from the gates, he came across two men, bound to chairs. They weren't like the others, so he knew they were both still alive. Both were staring sightlessly ahead. Heracles, intrigued, walked up to one of the men. Heracles obligingly broke apart the chains holding him, and lifted him out of the chair. The man frowned a little.

'Um, I've completely forgotten what I was doing,' the man said, wide-eyed. 'Do I know you?'

'I'm Heracles,' Heracles introduced himself.

The man frowned. 'I'm sure I know that name, but I can't remember.'

'What are you doing alive down in Hades?' Heracles asked.

'No idea,' the man replied.

Heracles looked at the chair. He knew it. The Chair of Forgetfulness. The man had probably been sitting in it for so long he'd forgotten how to remember. It would probably clear up. 'Don't worry,' he ended up saying, and reached forward to free the second man. But he'd barely moved within reaching distance before the ground suddenly shook badly, and he and the forgetful man both fell over.

'Oh, I forgot, you can't free him else the Underworld will collapse!' the forgetful man said.

Heracles looked at the man in the chair, realising there was no way he could free him. 'I'm sorry,' he said to the man in the chair, and looked at the forgetful man. 'What's your name?'

'I can't remember.'

'I'll call you Bobbodorus,' Heracles decided. 'Why are you in the Underworld, Bobbodorus?'

'We, um, we came to ... get something. Or someone? I think it was someone,' the man said, clearly thinking very hard.

'Who?'

'Um, a girl. Can't remember her name.'

'Good enough,' Heracles said, and gestured onwards. 'I've got to get Cerberus, then I'm going back up. You coming?'

'Um, sure,' Bobbodorus replied with a vague smile. 'Thanks … what was your name?'

'Heracles.'

'And what's my name?'

'Bobbodorus.'

'And where are we, again?'

Heracles sighed a little. 'Just follow me.'

Heracles and his new companion continued to the Gates of Hades, encountering many struggling souls on the way, and Heracles was never one to pass them by. He lifted the stone that Demeter had buried Ascalaphus under for telling her that her daughter, Persephone, was condemned to live in the Underworld, freeing the demon from his plight. He also wanted to give the souls blood, and slaughtered one of the kine of Hades to do so. This hadn't gone unnoticed, and a wrestling match with the cow's herder was only stopped by Persephone when Heracles was clearly about to kill him.

Finally, he reached Hades himself, who obviously had heard about Heracles being in his domain and leaving quite a trail of noticeable devastation in his wake.

'We are causing quite the ruckus, aren't we?' the god of the Underworld stated, his hands on his hips.

'Hades,' Heracles hailed. 'My name is...'

'Heracles, I know,' the god completed. 'And I also know that you're here to take Cerberus back to King Eurystheus.'

'Um, yeah,' Heracles replied, a little bashful.

'Well, I can't say I'm not rather impressed with your feats. I'll let you take Cerberus.'

'Oh, thanks!' Heracles said happily, somewhat relieved.

'But you need to do it without any weapons.'

Heracles frowned. 'Um, without weapons?'

'Yes, without weapons.'

'But that going to be impossible.'

'Oh, come on,' Hades said, 'I have to have *some* fun.'

Finally, Heracles reached Cerberus.

The dog was just as fearsome and terrifying as everyone had said. The rumours of the mutt's rather unique appearance were true. It was huge, with three angry heads, larger-than-necessary claws, a mane made of snakes, and a dragon in place of its tail. Even

Heracles was a little anxious as to how exactly he was supposed to subdue such a ferocious creature.

It barked madly at him, all three of its heads foaming at their mouths, with the black eyes of each head wide and crazy.

'There's a good doggy!' Heracles said quickly, his hands up in the air. 'Good boy!'

Cerberus didn't seem to care. It continued to bark and growl at Heracles, warning the hero of moving any closer.

'Sit! Lie down! Roll over! Play dead!' Heracles tried desperately as a means of subduing the beast, but clearly Cerberus hadn't been adequately trained, as it seemed to become even angrier at that. It launched a head forward to try and clamp its jaws on Heracles.

He just barely dodged it, and considered his options. As he was pondering, he looked over at Hades, who was sitting on a chair eating some bread, watching intently. He gave Heracles a little wave and a soundless cheer, pumping the air with his fist in support.

Heracles sighed, and turned back to the beast. There was only one thing for it. It was back to basics.

As one head launched forward to bite, Heracles grabbed it. Cerberus immediately tried to bite and scratch him as he was lifted into the air, its blood-chilling barks inches from Heracles' ears. However, the skin of the Nemean Lion that Heracles had acquired in his first labour repelled all of Cerberus' bites and swipes. He squeezed with all his might, like he had done with the Nemean Lion, but to his horror, Cerberus wasn't submitting.

He squeezed more with desperation, flailing a little. One of Heracles' legs came out from under the lion skin and immediately his leg surged with pain – the dragon in Cerberus' tail had bitten him. He pulled his leg back in and summoned every bead of strength he had within him to continue squeezing.

Eventually, Cerberus seemed to slow down, and his barks became less frequent and ferocious. Heracles didn't know how long he stayed there, holding the beast, until, finally, Cerberus relented and collapsed.

Heracles stumbled from the dog, checking his leg. There were signs of damage, but nothing too serious.

'Wow!' Hades exclaimed from the side, standing up and clapping. 'That was quite a show. Well done, Heracles. Let it never be said that Zeus fathered a half-human brutish nitwit.'

Heracles just gasped for air, nodding vaguely.

Hades walked up to Cerberus, patting it on one of its heads. 'There, there. You did well!'

The dog whined a little.

'Don't worry, you're still my favourite doggy, Cerby,' Hades said, scratching Cerberus behind one of his ears.

'Cerby?' Heracles repeated, still panting.

At the sound of his name Cerberus got up and stuck all three of his tongues out, panting and yapping, looking very happy.

'Now, you be a good doggy and go off with Heracles for a bit, and when you get back, I'll have your favourite dinner waiting for you!' Hades said. 'Battle-felled Spartan souls! Mmm! Yummy!'

Cerberus yapped again.

'Here you go, take his leash,' Hades said, giving Heracles a chain attached to the dog's necks. 'Now, take him and do whatever you wish. But I want him back. Deal?'

'Deal,' Heracles agreed, looking up at the now quite subdued beast, who was looking at Heracles with adorable, wide eyes.

'He always has a student of Heraclitanism for breakfast, he loves that,' Hades began, 'then it's a lovely walk around the river Oceanos that encircles the earth, then he likes a nice nap. Then in the afternoon he usually has one of the restless dead to gnaw on. After that, a quick dip in the Styx, and he's very content. But make sure you don't give him any Athenian statesmen; he can't stomach those, poor thing.'

'Err, got it,' Heracles said, raising an eyebrow slightly.

'See you in a while, Cerby!' Hades said.

Cerberus yapped happily again.

The man Heracles had dubbed Bobbodorus finally managed to recall his name as Theseus, but that was all he could remember – he was still suffering the effects of the chair when they ascended from the Underworld. Heracles set him on the road to Athens, and took himself and Cerberus back to meet King Eurystheus for the final time, summoning him to come to the city gates.

The look on the King's face was beyond priceless when he saw what Heracles had achieved.

'You ... you actually did it!?' the King yelped, hiding behind a wall just in case Cerberus attacked. 'But that's impossible!'

'Yep. Well, that's me done,' Heracles said without even acknowledging that. 'See you around, Eurystheus.'

'No, but wait!' the King said quickly, poking his head up from behind the wall. 'You have to perform another, because you ...'

'Oh, sod off,' Heracles said, and left to continue his story, full of intrigue, heroism, and adventure.

Hera was livid at the sheer incompetence of the King and the pain-in-the-Aristotle actions of her fellow gods and goddesses. Heracles was *still* alive, and he barely even had a mark to show for his fight with what was meant to be the most fearsome creature a man could confront.

She screamed so loudly with rage that Mount Olympus shook dramatically, waking up her husband.

'Hera?' Zeus called from another room. 'Would you mind keeping it down? Some of us are trying to take a nap!'

'Sorry, darling,' Hera said, forcing herself to sound calmer than she felt.

Zeus fell back to sleep quickly, and a chorus of godly snores resumed, each one causing a mild tremor of the mountain, leaving Hera to stew in her own bitter thoughts.

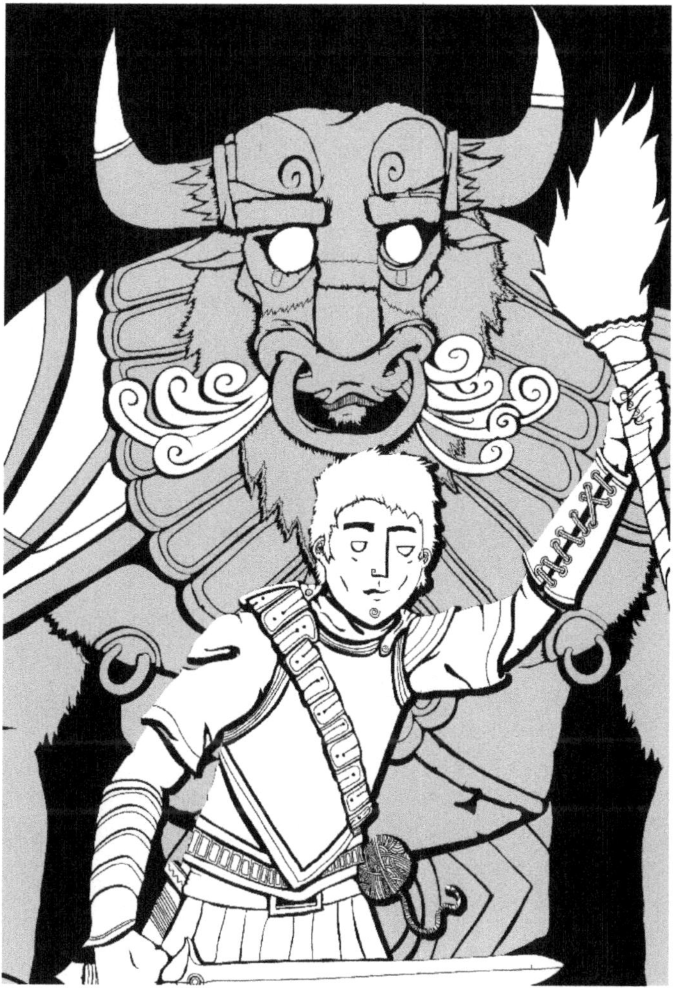

THE ADVENTURES OF YOUNG THESEUS

Theseus *loved* Heracles.

Raised by his mother and grandfather in a small village beyond Athens, he would often waylay travellers from the cities and ask them for news about his cousin's latest labour. He loved hearing about which beast Heracles had slayed or captured, squeezing every detail he could from the bemused travellers. He was always ecstatic when someone passed through that had met the man or been present at one of his fantastic deeds. By day, Theseus never stopped training and thinking about how much he wanted to be like Heracles, and by night, he dreamt of nothing but Heracles' awesome labours.

Theseus had almost met the great man once, when he was about seven years of age. Heracles had come to visit Theseus' grandfather, and laid aside his lion skin while he ate. Theseus had sneaked in with his friends, and at the sight of the lion skin, his friends had all fled. Assuming it to be alive, Theseus had relished his self-imposed labour and attacked the skin with his training sword. Of course, his blunt sword had achieved nothing, but little Theseus chose to remember it as the day he saved his village from the terrible lion, even if no one ever thanked him for it.

That only fuelled his ambition as he grew in age, strength, and intelligence under the counsel of his grandfather. He trained hard, aiming to one day emulate the deeds of his great hero, Heracles, and be heralded throughout the known world.

When he'd grown into a strong young man, his mother and his grandfather had taken him to a rock outside of the village. There, they told him about his lineage as the son of the King of Athens, and that many years ago, the King had left his sandals and sword under this rock. In order to prove himself as the king's heir, he should take them to Athens as tokens of his identity. In one swift flip of the heavy rock, he retrieved a nice pair of boots and a dulled sword, left by the king.

His mother was in floods of tears. 'Oh, my little boy, all grown up!' she said. 'I've so dreaded this day!'

'It's okay, mum, 'cause I'm gonna be a hero!' Theseus informed her happily.

She smiled. 'Now, I've packed all your favourite foods; your chlamys tunic so you can go hunting; your himation in case you get cold; your short chiton; your long chiton; your dress chiton; your best chiton; a few peronei fasteners to keep you looking smart; your petasus hat; your bow and your arrows; your xiphos sword; your dagger; your kopis sword; your lucky sheathe; and a spare pair of perizoma in case you get run over by a chariot.'

She handed him a very large bag that looked so full that it seemed ready to burst. Theseus, despite his great strength, nearly fell over.

'Thanks, Mum,' Theseus said, heaving the bag onto his back.

'Now,' she said, and nodded to Theseus' grandfather standing next to her. 'Your grandfather and I agreed that you should go to Athens by sea.'

'Can't I go by land?' Theseus asked, disappointed.

'The land route is dangerous, full of thieves and miscreants!' his mother told him.

'But mum!' Theseus complained. 'While Heracles is out there doing his labours, how can I be a hero if I take the safe route? And I can't go and meet my father and bring him an unbloodied sword! He'll think I'm a right wet fish!'

'The road to Athens is highly dangerous, my boy,' his grandfather told him. 'There's a club-wielding maniac; a bandit nicknamed the Pine-Bender who kills people by ripping them apart with pine trees; a fearsome sow; a man who kicks people off of cliffs; a man who kills by wrestling; and a strange old man who chops off people's feet.'

'I forbid you to take the road!' his mother said.

'But that's not fair!' Theseus complained. 'You never let me do what I want!'

His mother and grandfather looked at each other. They weren't going to talk him out of it.

The road to Athens was every bit as dramatic and life-endangering as his mother and grandfather had warned him.

He was first assaulted by the club-wielding maniac, Periphetes. Theseus took the task of killing him very seriously, and dispensed the foe without too much trouble. Reminded of Heracles' infamous club, Theseus took the club and made it his main weapon. From that point on, he endeavoured to serve these evil people the same violence they wished to do to him. That's what Heracles would do, after all.

Next, he killed Sinis the Pine-Bender with the bandit's own grizzly methods, by ripping him apart through tying him to two pine trees, despite Theseus not knowing how the contraption even worked.

After that he had a small moral dilemma to think over. Although he hadn't yet met the fearsome sow his grandfather had mentioned, he reasoned that to be a true hero like Heracles, he shouldn't just kill villainous men in self-defence; he should also seek them out. So, he went a little out of his way to hunt down the Crommyonian sow, and killed her too.

That was followed by meeting Sciron – the one who encouraged passers-by to wash his feet before kicking them off the cliff into the sea to be devoured by a huge turtle. Theseus enthusiastically grabbed his feet and threw him to the turtle instead.

Then came the challenge of Cercyon, the wrestler. Theseus dutifully out-wrestled him and killed him too, barely breaking a sweat.

His last deed on the road to Athens came in the creepy form of Procrustes, a terrifying individual who would offer hospitality to travellers. He'd make them lie down, and if they didn't fit the bed perfectly, he would stretch them if they were too short, or chop off their feet if they were too tall. Theseus, just like all the enemies before this one, gave him his just desserts by chopping off Procrustes' feet instead when it turned out he was too tall for his own bed.

Finally, Theseus arrived at Athens. His father's sword was bloody, his new club a bit battered, and he was truly gleeful about his string of accomplishments. He strolled into the city proudly, sticking out his chest. It was a world away from the village he'd grown up in – bustling crowds, new noises that nearly deafened him, new smells assaulting his nostrils - everything his small village never had. He was almost overwhelmed by it all. It was common in his village to greet every passer-by, but he realised in this hectic environment that people didn't tend to do the same in a city.

He decided to eat and rest before going to his father. To his woe, he heard the townsfolk talking about his father now living with Medea – the witch who tended to leave a string of magical murders in her wake – with the condition that she give the King an heir. This had left his father's household in shambles, and the people of Athens in confusion and dissent.

Once he'd heard all he'd needed to, Theseus decided to go to his father to tell him the great news that he already had an heir who was alive and well, and that he could get rid of murderous witch. He'd surprise him, he decided, and headed to the palace.

Medea, through her magical powers, had sensed the presence of Theseus in the city, and knew what he intended to do. She simply couldn't let that happen. If the King knew he already had an heir, he would no longer need her. Theseus would push her out, back into desolation.

She quickly decided on a plan. It was her favourite kind of plan. She had to kill Theseus.

When Theseus arrived at the palace, she stood stoically by her husband's side. The young, strong, handsome man walked confidently up to the King, and dropped to one knee courteously. He then cleared his throat, and began a well-prepared speech:

'My liege, my name is Theseus. I've travelled from the village of Troezen, along the dangerous road to Athens, full of evil men and beasts. I've killed them all in the ways they intended to do me harm, all to have an audience with you.'

'Oh, excellent,' King Aegeus said, smiling. 'What can I do for you, young man?'

Theseus' hand began to move. Medea knew there was some trick he was about to play to prove his lineage.

'My liege,' she interrupted, causing Theseus to hesitate. 'I feel this young man has wild stories to tell. Perhaps we should invite him to tonight's banquet so he could regale us?'

'What an excellent idea,' the King replied, smiling. 'Theseus, please join us tonight for our banquet.'

'I'd be honoured,' Theseus replied, and left.

Medea waited until the young man had departed before she leaned into her husband.

'My King, you must kill this Theseus,' she hissed into his ear.

The King looked at her, confused. 'But he seemed like a polite, upwardly mobile young man.'

'He seeks to take your throne!' she said.

'Does he?' the King asked, confused.

'I hear him and his vile thoughts about you, the power he craves!' she coaxed the king. 'You must dispense with him before he can strike, lest you lose Athens to this vile man!'

King Aegeus looked at her. 'Are you sure?'

'Positive, my King!' Medea said.

He nodded slowly. 'Then I will kill him.'

'Replace his wine with poison, my King,' Medea stated. 'Then he shall sip, and as he dies you shall declare your reign is everlasting, your power is infinite, that no one should dare to usurp you.'

Theseus knew how to act at a banquet, thanks to his grandfather's lessons. He did everything his grandfather had taught him - performing all the little rituals and customs these people liked. He knew to be a worthy son of the king he needed to be not only strong and clever, but also polite and familiar with the ways of royalty. Even though he was buzzing with excitement about what was going to happen, he kept calm and collected, and projected the outward appearance of a mighty hero.

After bathing, he entered the banquet hall, dressed in his finest chiton, with his father's sandals, and the sword in his lucky sheath. The hall itself was so magnificent it completely blew him away. Elaborately decorated, with statues of the gods, and finely-embroidered cloths draping expensive sofas laid out in a pleasing arrangement around a huge table. There was chatting from plenty of rich-looking man, all in glorious outfits, all projecting deeply noble appearances.

As was custom, he greeted his hosts. He was then shown the highly honourable seat next to the King, where a slave removed his sandals and purified his feet to cleanse them of the dust from the street. Theseus then reclined in the accepted manner, leaning with his left arm on a cushion, leaving his right hand free. He watched as the other guests all milled around, deciding he could get very used to this.

The slaves then brought in the food. Mountains of the best meats, with vegetables and dipping sauces. Theseus knew the custom was not to drink or converse, so the gathering consumed these in silence. This was followed by dessert – cakes, fruit, and pastries of the finest quality.

Once the meal was complete, the room was cleared and the drinks arrived by the gallon for the evening's carousal, along with some more cakes.

He was pleased when his father immediately engaged him in conversation, along with a few nobles.

'You must tell us about your exploits, young Theseus,' the king said. 'I'm keen to hear of your wild deeds.'

'Of course, my King,' Theseus said, about to open his mouth to explain his adventures on the way to Athens, when his father stopped him.

'But before that, you must drink this fine wine,' he said, proffering a cup of wine to the young man. Theseus took it.

'Thank you,' Theseus said. This was his moment, he decided. 'Many evils on the road I had to cut aside with my trusty sword.' He drew his sword casually, showing it to the King. To look even more casual, he raised the cup of wine to his mouth, ready to sip ...

'Stop!' the King suddenly roared, hitting the cup out of Theseus' hand. It fell to the floor with a clang, where its contents hissed and spat, gnawing away at the fine mosaic.

Shocked, Theseus blinked. 'Um, what?' he asked, realising everyone was now staring at them.

'Your sword!' the King cried.

Theseus grinned. 'Father, I have come to take my place by you. I swear to perform mighty deeds and cut down the most evil of –'

'Medea!' his father suddenly roared, ruining Theseus' well-prepared speech.

'The most evil of men, and ...' Theseus tried to continue, but realised his father wasn't listening to him – he was looking around the room, his eyes full of fury and hatred, searching for the witch Medea. There was suddenly a rush of footsteps as Medea swept out of the room in a blur of fine-embroidery.

'Find that witch and kill her!' King Augeas demanded of his soldiers, who pursued Medea immediately. He then turned to Theseus. 'You carry my sword, Theseus. Who is your mother?'

'My mother is Aethra, my King.'

The king's eyes widened. 'Theseus, are you my son!?'

Everyone around them gasped. Theseus, despite everything. decided he was going to enjoy this moment. He straightened up, puffed out his chest, and put on his best heroic face. 'Yes, father, it is me!'

'I have an heir!' the king realised with joy, and swept the young man up in a hug. 'Oh, I thought this day would never arrive! Theseus, my blood, my son!'

'Yeah!' Theseus managed to squeak out from the vice-like hug of his father.

King Aegeus, crying with joy, finally let go of the crushed Theseus and turned to the crowd. 'Noble people of Athens, hear this! I declare this strong, clever, and noble young man to be my blood son, and the heir to Athens!'

Still slightly shocked, the crowd finally thought to celebrate with cheers, just as a soldier came rushing back in to the gathering.

'My king!' the soldier cried. 'We couldn't stop the witch! She escaped in a chariot pulled by dragons before we had a chance!'

'No matter, the evil witch flees!' King Aegeus declared triumphantly. 'Friends,' the king continued, wrapping an arm around Theseus' shoulders. 'Tonight, we shall honour the gods like never before! We shall sing the name of Dionysus as we drink, dance, and be merry, for I have an heir!'

Time passed.

Being the heir to Athens was great and he was happy, but it was a little boring for Theseus. Since arriving, he hadn't done much in the way of being a hero, and with every passing moment he spent in splendour, his thoughts turned to Heracles. All the while Theseus was sitting here, living in luxury, Heracles was out there performing his labours. The last Theseus had heard of Heracles, he'd retrieved the man-eating mares of Diomedes, and what had Theseus done? Eat grapes.

He decided soon after that he couldn't just sit here being a prince. He needed excitement, and he needed to show the people of Athens that he was a worthy and strong heir to the kingdom. He needed his own personal labour to complete.

After asking around, Theseus discovered, to his absolute delight, that the product of one of Heracles' labours, the Cretan bull, had been set free by Heracles and was now roaming around Tetrapolis, doing no small mischief to the people. This was his chance, he decided.

His father tried to tell him not to worry about it, but he insisted. He packed up and headed out the region of Tetrapolis - specifically Marathon, where the bull was rumoured to live.

On the way, a horrendous storm began to rage. Seeking refuge, Theseus knocked on the door of a lone house. It was answered by a frail old woman.

'Hi, I'm Theseus,' the young man said boldly. 'I'm looking for cover from the storm.'

The old woman gazed at him for a moment before her face suddenly erupted into a beautiful smile. 'Well, come in, come in. You'll catch a cold if you stand out there, child!'

She stepped aside to allow him entry. He stepped into a modest settling, without much in the way of value, but with a lot of personal assets.

'Now you sit yourself there and dry off, and I'll fetch some sweets,' the old woman said, ushering Theseus to a seat by the fire. 'Zeus may be angry, but that doesn't mean we can't have cake!'

As the storm raged outside, Theseus and the old woman, Hecale, stayed warm and safe inside her house, chatting. Theseus told her all about himself and his mission, and she in turn told him many anecdotes she'd amassed over her life. She even regaled the eager Theseus about the time she'd seen Heracles. He dearly hoped he would meet the man himself one day.

When the storm finally subsided, Theseus made ready to leave.

'Now, you wrap up warm – you can't capture a bull when you're freezing with cold, child!' Hecale said, making sure his himation was well-adjusted on him. 'I hate to think what your mother would say if she knew you were killing a legendary bull without wrapping up warm!'

Theseus nodded, smiling at her. 'Thanks, Hecale.'

'Don't you worry yourself, child!' Hecale said happily. 'And please, don't be a stranger. If you succeed, return here, so I can sacrifice to Zeus. I'll wait right here for you!'

Theseus' smiled broadened. A sacrifice, just like Heracles' first labour, he thought. 'I will. See you later, Hecale.'

'Good bye!'

Theseus had been keen for a challenge, so when capturing the bull proved to be painfully easy, it was a little disappointing. He rode the bull as Heracles had, through the city of Marathon, to the delight of the crowds, and then back to Hecale's house, keen to show the lovely old lady his success.

However, there was no activity around the house when he arrived. He knocked on the door, but there was no answer. She had said she'd wait, and he hadn't been gone that long.

'Hecale?' he called, and stuck his head through a window. What he saw made his heart sink.

There, lying on the floor, unmoving, was Hecale. The old lady had died before he could return.

He wept for her loss.

After he'd returned to Athens to a hero's welcome and sacrificed the bull to the gods, things went back to being very quiet. As soon everyone stopped talking about his deed, and he was searching for his next one. As far as he was concerned, he was still very far away from matching Heracles.

When a fleet of ships with black sails arrived from Crete, Theseus jumped with excitement at the prospect of fighting for his kingdom and his people. But when his father did nothing but look sad as the Cretans strolled into the city, meeting no resistance, Theseus was very, very confused. He asked his father what was going on.

'One of my regrets,' his father began, looking down from the palace to the piazza where the Cretans were gathering and where the people of Athens were protesting, 'is this foul contract we have with Minos.'

'The king of Crete?' Theseus asked, puzzled. 'What's the contract? Why do the people of Athens hate you?'

'Many years ago, his son was murdered in our streets, at my command. Minos came to seek satisfaction for his death. But we ignored him, to our peril. Minos waged war on Athens and sought the fury of the gods. He got it. Greece was afflicted with drought and famine. Our crops were destroyed.

'We were desperate. All of Greece prayed to the god Aeacus for relief – the drought ceased for the rest of Greece, but it continued to plague Athens. We asked Aeacus how we might escape our perils. He told us we must do whatever Minos asked of us.

'King Minos has the Minotaur, kept in a labyrinth in Crete. Every nine years he sends ships here to fetch seven youths and seven maidens to feed it, for as long as the Minotaur lives. We must give him what he wants, lest we be plagued again.'

Theseus swallowed nervously. 'We have to break this cycle,' he stated.

'The only solution is the death of the minotaur,' his father told him. 'But those that go into the labyrinth where it dwells either get lost and die, or are killed by the Minotaur.'

Theseus nodded. 'Then I'll kill it.'

His father looked at him, horrified. 'Theseus, this isn't some road bandit or a bull. This is the Minotaur – a hybrid form of monstrous shape, born of a woman and the Cretan bull. In total, we have sent twenty-eight sacrifices at King Minos' demand. Some of the youths were our best fighters and thinkers. Not one has returned to us. All have died.'

'Dad,' Theseus stated firmly, straightening up. 'You can't keep doing this. Someone needs to kill it. I'll do it, okay?'

His father suddenly became angry, like Theseus had never seen before. 'Theseus, you are the sole heir to Athens, and I shall not allow you to die so pointlessly! I forbid you!'

'But it's not pointless!' Theseus protested. 'Yeah, I'm the heir to Athens, but what does that mean if I don't act to protect my people? Fourteen of our people have to die every nine years? Plus, this all your fault, Dad. How can you just stand there and stop me from going when the people have gotta pay for a murder you ordered? They're losing their sons and daughters because of what you did. They hate you. How long can you rule a kingdom that hates you?'

His father fell silent.

'I'll join the sacrifice, kill the Minotaur and return,' Theseus said after a moment of deathly silence. He made to leave, but his father stopped him.

'Theseus,' he said sadly, his eyes shining. 'You are all I have. I beg of you not to go.'

'I'm sorry, Dad.'

His father sighed, bowing his head. 'Very well. But my boy, promise me one thing.'

'What?'

'Should you succeed in killing the Minotaur, change your sails from black to white, so I might know your fate as the ship sails to Athens.'

Theseus nodded, and offered him a smile. 'I promise.'

Then he left.

After praying to the gods for good fortune in his task, Theseus and the thirteen other youths and maidens that had been selected by lottery sailed to Crete. Theseus was overjoyed to be following in Heracles' footsteps. Once there, they were escorted to the palace and greeted by King Minos and his beautiful daughter, Ariadne, standing by his side. Theseus could barely take his eyes off her.

'I pity your fate, young ones,' King Minos said sincerely to them all. 'But this is the debt your king owes. Tonight, we shall wine and dine greatly for your last meal before your passage to the Elysian Fields. I should like to allow you the courteously of speaking with each of you individually and learn your names and ways before I send you in this dire task.'

So, Theseus and his fellow Athenians were entertained by the King and his daughter. It wasn't long before Theseus' identity came to light and King Minos came to see him.

'The foreign son of King Aegeus, well, I never,' King Minos said. 'The man is less cowardly than I thought, to send his only heir.'

'I chose to come, sir,' Theseus said, looking at the beautiful Ariadne by her father's side. He straightened up a little, puffing up his chest, hoping to impress her. 'I'm going to slay the Minotaur.'

'Are you, now?' the king asked, slightly bemused. 'No man has yet to returned alive to speak of his encounter.'

'Then I'll be the first,' Theseus replied casually.

There was brief pause as the king took that in. The people around them had fallen silent, some of them giggling at Theseus.

'You are a fool, boy, just like your father,' the king scoffed.

'Or a hero,' Theseus posited.

The king snorted with laughter, and walked away.

'Do you really plan to kill the Minotaur?' Ariadne asked as the crowd around them resumed their chat.

Theseus nodded. 'For my dad, and for my people.'

'You're so brave,' Ariadne said, all in a fluster.

Theseus puffed out his chest a bit more. He really needed to impress her. 'It's just what I do,' he told her.

She suddenly glanced around them, checking for any eavesdroppers. 'Theseus, please let me help you.'

'Help me?' Theseus asked, startled.

'The problem with the labyrinth isn't just the Minotaur, it's also the labyrinth itself,' she said. 'You might be able to kill it, but you'll never find your way out again.'

'So ... what should I do?' Theseus asked.

'Meet me tonight in the grounds,' she said, and with that, she went back to her father.

Theseus watched her go, transfixed by her beauty. He decided that when he came back from the labyrinth, he was going to ask her if she fancied going to the amphitheatre together.

After doing his hair and straightening his chiton so he looked his best, he met Ariadne in the grounds later that night, as she'd asked. She looked very pleased to see him.

'I'm so glad you came,' she said, smiling. 'Thank you, Theseus.'

'You're welcome,' he said, puffing out his chest again, like a bird showing off its plumage. 'What d'you wanna talk about?'

'The Minotaur is a plague to us. It is a constant reminder to my father of my mother's bewitching and the day she gave birth to it,' she said.

Theseus raised an eyebrow. 'Wait ... the Minotaur is technically your step-brother?'

She looked a bit bashful. 'Yeah.'

'Oh, awkward,' Theseus murmured. They had some serious issues on Crete, he mused.

'Anyway, I went to see Daedalus, the one who created the labyrinth,' she said, 'and I know exactly what you need to do.'

Theseus' eyes widened. 'What?'

'But before I tell you, promise me something.'

'Sure?'

She paused momentarily, dropping her gaze to the ground. 'Marry me, take me back to Athens, and I'll have your babies.'

Theseus' jaw dropped. He could feel his ears burning. '... Err, in that order?' he asked eventually.

She giggled in reply. She looked even more beautiful when she giggled, Theseus thought. After the shock subsided a little, he nodded.

'I will, I promise,' he said, bowing courteously to her.

She nodded in return, and held out a ball of string to him before telling him exactly what he needed to do.

Theseus, despite knowing the dangers, was in high spirits they were made to go inside the labyrinth. He managed to shoot a secret smile at Ariadne, who offered one back.

It was dark, but not dark enough to blind him, as he had a lit torch. He dared to venture forward slightly, trying to get an understanding of how the labyrinth was constructed. There were many thin corridors made of stone, with about ten paths branching off from where he was stood, all looking exactly the same. He knew each of those corridors broke into their own ten paths, which then broke into ten more, and so on. It would be impossible to navigate this labyrinth by eye alone.

Fortunately, he didn't have to.

He did exactly what Ariadne had told him to do. He tied the end of the string to the entrance, and allowed it to unravel as he walked, following the path she had instructed him to take.

He was there for a long time, searching for the beast. Eventually, the Minotaur appeared out of the shadows. Theseus had never seen a creature like it. Half-man, half-bull, its nostrils flared as it spotted him and grunted, stamping its hoof. Then, it charged, horns down, straight towards him.

Theseus immediately dropped the remainder of the ball of string and jumped aside, deftly dodging the Minotaur before it crashed headlong into the wall behind Theseus, cracking the stone. It turned back, completely unaffected, its horns as strong and sharp as ever as Theseus jogged backwards to put distance between them.

'Come at me!' Theseus goaded, readying himself again. The Minotaur charged. This time when Theseus sidestepped he reached up to its horn, caught it, and with his combined strength and the Minotaur's charging force, ripped the horn clean out of the Minotaur's head. It crashed into the other wall.

It roared, angered, and came at him a third time. Theseus deftly cut its leg quite severely with its own horn before it crashed yet again into the wall.

It was *really* angry now, and slowed and dazed by its repeated collisions with the wall. It charged once more. This time, just before it reached him, Theseus stood his ground, statue-like. As they met, Theseus strafed to the right, launched himself spectacularly off the wall and onto the Minotaur's back as it passed. He then wrapped his arms around the mighty beast's neck, and squeezed as hard as he could. The Minotaur struggled wildly, trying to throw Theseus off, but to no avail. It could do nothing as Theseus kept tightening his grip, his teeth gritted with the effort. Then, finally, the Minotaur's neck cracked, and the terrifying beast collapsed to the ground, dead.

Theseus got up, only slightly out of breath. He cautiously considered the creature and tentatively kicked it. The beast didn't move.

Grinning, he pulled his father's sword out of the creature and picked up his string. Once he'd found the Athenians he'd come with, all he had to do was follow the string back to the entrance.

When the night drew in, he and the Athenians emerged from the labyrinth in secret. He instructed the young Athenians to get to their ship, whilst he went to retrieve Ariadne.

She was beyond elated to see him, kissing him in love, admiration, and pure relief. She was already packed to go, so they secretly left the palace and headed back to the ship.

They started on their journey back to Athens, but it soon became clear that a storm was moving in. Theseus ordered that they make landfall on an island and wait for the storm to subside. There, he, Ariadne, and the joyous young Athenians celebrated, singing Dionysus' name as they drank, ate, and celebrated the simple pleasure of still being alive. They were all quite surprised when, after singing his name so much in a drunken haze, the god Dionysus appeared to them, his smile stretching from ear to ear.

'Whoa man, we got a party going on up in here!' Dionysus said happily, staggering to where the wine was and helping himself to a cup. 'Beach party! I love that man, that's awesome! Everyone's gotta do a beach party!'

Before anyone could say anything, he spotted a face among the crowd he recognised, turning abruptly and knocking over all of the drinks, nearly falling over backwards in the process. 'Dude, Kadmos! I ain't see you since your fifth birthday party! Where you been at, bro?'

'Err ...' Kadmos began, but Dionysus had already been side-tracked.

'Hey girl, you wanna ...' he said to someone with long hair. The person turned, and Dionysus saw the beard immediately. 'It's a dude, bro!' Dionysus realised, and laughed. With everyone watching him, he walked drunkenly across the gathered circle and practically fell between Theseus and and Ariadne.

'Excuse me, but ...' Theseus began.

'Theseus! You know how to throw a party!' Dionysus cried, slapping him on the back with misjudged strength, sending Theseus falling forward into the sand headfirst.

Dionysus laughed uproariously. 'Oh my Zeus! I'm so sorry, bro! Lemme help you ... oh.' He suddenly stopped as he saw the beautiful Ariadne, staring at him with wide, terrified eyes. 'Hello, pretty lady,' he said, smiling. 'What's your pretty name?' he asked, before laughing at his own unintended joke.

'Ariadne ...' Ariadne said nervously.

'Dionysus!' Theseus tried to interrupt, trying to get between the god and princess. But in one swift movement Dionysus knocked him back down to the ground again.

'Let's get married!' Dionysus cried, taking her arm, and with Ariadne's cry of surprise and anguish, they both disappeared in a puff of godly smoke.

Theseus, still on the ground, could only stare at the space Ariadne had been sitting. No one else dared to speak as he remained silent, speechless and heartbroken. He felt completely numb. For a good while, he didn't move – just stared.

When the storm subsided and they continued on to Athens, Theseus no longer felt the joy of accomplishing his labour. His only feeling was despair for the loss of his love. He was so sad he forgot the change his sails, as his father had made him promise.

The ship got within sight of Athens, with its sails still black.

King Aegeus had been waiting, looking out to sea from the Acropolis of Athens, tense with anxiety and fear for the fate of his son and heir. He stood stoically, moving for nothing, waiting to see the ship that he hoped would bring his son home, safe and well.

Finally, a ship appeared on the horizon. He strained to see its sails, his heart racing. After a few minutes, they came into focus.

They were black.

His son was dead.

He dropped to his knees, howling in grief. The young man he'd only just come to know - his son, his heir, the boy he cherished so dearly - had been killed by the Minotaur.

Despairing, he ascended the rock of the Acropolis and threw himself from the top.

Meanwhile, Theseus stood on the ship facing away from the sails, oblivious to his father's fate. The ship continued slowly into port, through the body of water that, in time, would come to be known the Aegean Sea.

Upon his arrival in Athens, Theseus discovered the death of his father, and grieved bitterly for his oversight in not changing his sails. However, the people were overjoyed by his slaying of the Minotaur, saving their sons and daughters from the cycle of sacrifices.

Despite the loss of both his love and his father, Theseus couldn't help but feel proud of himself for all he had achieved in a few short years. His slaying of the Minotaur would be spoken of for years to come, just like the labours of Heracles. Finally, he was a hero, and maybe one day - if he was very lucky - he would meet the mighty Heracles, and they would be able to swap their epic stories, as equals.

That would be a day, he thought, which he would never forget.

With a new smile on his face, King Theseus of Athens took his place, and readied himself. After all, his next heroic adventure wouldn't be far away.

ABOUT THE AUTHOR

'Loves to imagine a lot of things that never happened and write them down so other people can too.'

Born in Essex and raised in Devon, England, Emily Templar is a self-confessed geek and avid cat lover. Her writing beginnings bloomed after visit from Michael Morpurgo OBE to speak to her class, during which five-year-old Emily decided she wanted to be an author just like Mr Morpurgo. She swiftly went on her way, to a life of typing continually into word processors.

Seemingly half-human, half-computer, she's been posting her work online to judgemental strangers since the age of eleven, and she published her first novel, *Zeek Kim'lo: The Fifth Best Detective Agency in the Universe*, whilst studying a for an honours degree in 'Liberal Arts: Ancient History with Proficiency in Japanese' at the University of Exeter.

She was a regional chess champion at the age of twelve, and she is a winner of a national television quiz show, 'The Chase'. She has produced an album with Randy Bachman, was in the television audience that saw Mo Farah win 'The Cube', and has been lost in the ITV studios where she ended up having a chinwag with a popular chat show host in the café.

Now a Freelance Writer, Emily continues to write and publish her original works alongside her vague attempts at adulting.

MORE FROM THIS AUTHOR

Zeek Kim'lo: The Fifth Best Detective Agency in the Universe

ISBN-13: 978-1530945078 / ISBN-10: 1530945070

The Zeek Kim'lo Detective Agency are officially the Fifth Best Detective Agency in the Universe, just behind the Singing Mice Detective Agency of Joomla District 3 (they had a good year). In order to win first place at the Best Awards, the Zeek Kim'lo Agency must dare to take on the most dangerous of cases … the trouble is, nobody thinks they're any good.

Zeek's agency are called to the murder of an innocent pet, but become the witnesses of an armed robbery at the planetary museum. Thrown abruptly into the murderous world of a massive criminal gang, Zeek and his employees must solve the case, whilst saving their own lives.

OUT NOW

COMING SOON

Zeek Kim'lo: Still the Fifth Best Detective Agency in the Universe

'I'm a spy. A government spy.' Zeek stared at him with wide eyes. '... Um, what?' 'Please, we have little time,' the prydanian said, holding his side and grunting in pain. 'There may be a plot currently in place that could result in the destruction of this entire continent. The perpetrator must be discovered and prevented from carrying out their plan. Will you help, Zeek Kim'lo?'

The Zeek Kim'lo Detective Agency fall into the world of espionage when Zeek discovers a safe house of Prydan's Intelligence Agency, containing their most adept spy. The destruction of the continent appears to be imminent, and it seems that the only people who can save it are the Fifth Best Detective Agency in the Universe.

Providence Street

The year is 2218. Technological advancements have given humanity a chance to go beyond the Earth to find sanctuary on other planets, in the beginnings of the human galactic empire. Those on the Earth are now used to encountering robots daily, doing jobs that their great grandparents used to do.

In south-west England, there are thirty dwellings on Providence Street. These are some of their stories.